DEATH BY CARROTS

A WIZARD DETECTIVE PARANORMAL ROMANCE

KARIN DE HAVIN

Death by Umbrella is coming in July!

The Shifter Vampire Alliance Serial

The Shifter Vampire Alliance features Derrick Dunne and takes place in the same world as The Wizard Detective Series.

Episodes 1-7 are complete!

Join Karin's newsletter for the *Baking with Books* recipes and receive a free short story!

Click here to join Karin's newsletter!

KARIN'S SERIES
**INDICATES FINISHED SERIES **

If you like Harry Potter with genies, read...
The Genie Academy**
If you like Twilight with wizards, read...
The Girl Chameleon**
If you like The Hunger Games set in Heaven, read...
Nine Lives Part One**
If you like Buffy the Vampire Slayer, read...
How to Snag a Shifter**
If you like books set in foreign lands with ghosts, read...
Tokyo Academy-First Contact**
If you like happily ever after time travel romances, read...
Jin In Time Part One**
If you like books that take place in the world of celebrities and fashion with a fantasy twist, read...
Celebrity Witch**

To Dave: Who can deduce I need a snack to keep writing better than anyone!
To Sammy: You are the cutest sidekick until you bring me a centipede.
To Storm: My very own book dragon who thought Derrick deserved his very own series. You were right!

1

AN ORDINARY DAY UNTIL...

Cruising down the 405 freeway for the three hundredth time, I wish I could put my magical powers to use. As a wizard of the Twelfth Order, instead of traveling by car in bumper-to-bumper traffic, I could just as easily teleport. Of course, that would be breaking a major wizarding rule. I still had a few more years and many more pages in my spellbook to complete before I could use the teleportation spell without the permission of my boss—the Exemplary Wizard.

I patted the leather covered steering wheel of my trusty jet-black 5 series sedan. My cover as a Zoomer driver working reconnaissance for the Twelfth Order meant my BMW was an integral part of my life. The center screen blinks signaling a text coming in. It looks like my regular client needs a ride cross town. I jerk the wheel hard and pop off at the next exit. With the aid of a bit of wizard magic, in ten minutes I pull up to the curb of my client's Wilshire West Spanish style apartment building.

Krissy beams as she struts down the concrete sidewalk like the runway model she is. "Hey, Der, long time no see."

I chuckle, knowing I'd given her a ride last night. "Amazing how much you've changed. Must be a full moon coming up." It is our running joke. Krissy is not only an up-and-coming model, but a werewolf.

Krissy positions herself in the back seat making sure she didn't give me a free show as her mini dress creeps up her thighs. "Very funny. You know I still have three weeks to go."

I love being the go-to Zoomer driver for the paranormals that inhabit Los Angeles. Not that I don't drive ordinary people as well, but the conversations are much more fun when I chat with my fellow paranormals. In a town where secrets barely last an hour before they are splashed all over the internet, it feels good to have a true secret from the rest of the LA world.

"WHERE TO?" I ASK WHILE KRISSY'S THUMBS FLY across her phone.

Without taking her eyes off her phone for a second, she says, "I have a photo shoot at Chateau Marmont."

I nod, knowing the way to the famous hotel in the Hollywood Hills all too well. The replica of a French chateau is a favorite spot not only for social climbers, but also for a few of my paranormal friends. The bar, with its dark romantic lighting, is the perfect place for them to blend in with the crowd, and an exclusive one at that.

"Are you shooting by the pool area? It's so old school."

Krissy finishes up her text, pushes her long blonde hair behind her ears, and graces me with one of her highly in demand pouty half smiles. "Of course, where else? Ron never misses an opportunity to get me into a bikini. I think there are far better pools in Hollywood, but he loves all the mature trees and the greenery edging the pool. He's obsessed with the Chateau towers. They are always looming in the background."

The benefit of having Krissy as a regular customer is the fact that I know exactly who Ron is—an A class jerk fashion photographer who works for Harper's magazine. "I don't know why you work with that creep. But he seems to request you a lot."

Her pout turns into a full-fledged smile. "Yeah, he's kind of into me. My pheromones drive him crazy."

The werewolf pheromones she is so proud of have zero effect on me. No one could replace my long-lost witch fiancée Tara.

Krissy eyes me in the rear-view mirror. "Why the glum face, Der? You're too handsome to be depressed."

I feign a half smile, appreciating her flattery. "Sorry, I was thinking of a painful memory."

"How long has it been since your fiancé died?"

Did everyone in the paranormal world know about my tragic love life? I sigh. "A year in September."

Instead of looking sad for me she beams. "I heard you roasted the vamp that killed her real good."

I wince. Talk about a memory I didn't want to revisit. "And here I thought witches were the worst gossips."

She chuckles. "They are. But we female werewolves are a close second."

Krissy's sense of humor brightens my mood a bit. "I'll keep that in mind."

She leans forward and gives my suit jacket shoulder pad a squeeze. "It's time for you to get back out there."

I wince a second time. The thought of dating again sends a chill down my back. I turn onto Sunset Boulevard and inch along until I hit the white painted brick walls that surround the Chateau Marmont. "Thanks for caring, but I'm good."

I pull up to the curb of the hotel. "Oh darn, it's your stop."

Killing the engine, I race over to open the door for her. She leans over flashing me a bit of her perfect natural cleavage, then gently kisses my cheek. "I know a lot of nice girls that would love to go on a date with you Der, me included. Text when you're ready."

I watch her hips as they sway back and forth, noticing how her satin blue mini dress strategically covers her butt by two inches. Krissy is a beautiful woman any guy would kill to date—just not this guy. A tall, dark-haired man holds the door open for her. She gives him a quick nod and then vanishes inside the hotel. I see several men and a few women still staring after Krissy. She certainly has quite the group of admirers.

Getting back inside my car, I know I'll never join

her fan club. My heart is sealed up tight. The woman who could open it back up doesn't exist—not anymore.

THE SCREEN FLASHES A CALENDAR REMINDER THAT MY meeting at Twelfth Order Headquarters is in thirty minutes. Once again, I wish I could use the transportation spell. The Order Headquarters is clear across town. It will take more than a little sleight of hand magic to make it to the meeting on time. My boss, the Exemplary Wizard, has a thing about tardiness. Late is the last thing I need to be when I'm vying for a new position. Not that being a Zoomer driver who secretly cruises around Los Angeles fixing things before they become disasters isn't quite exciting at times. Yet, after three years in the position it has somehow become mundane.

My phone buzzes and the unmistakable face of Mr. Kumar, the Exemplary Wizard's right-hand man, pops up on the screen. I smile as I take in his striking silk purple jacket. A wonderful compliment to his jet-black hair and his mocha-colored skin. I take in his large brown eyes and know why the women in the Order find him as handsome as a Bollywood star.

In his impeccable British accented voice, he says, "Greetings, Derrick. I wanted to speak to you before the meeting."

This could either be good news or bad. "Yes, sir." I grip the steering wheel tightly and grimace. "I'm ready."

His deep baritone laugh fills the car. "Don't worry, it's not bad news. In fact, I think you will be quite pleased."

Unfortunately, I know Mr. Kumar all too well. He is not going to tell me what the good news might be. He loves to string things out to produce the most dramatic effect. "I can't wait to find out at the meeting."

Mr. Kumar's brow furrows. "By my calculations you are going to be approximately twenty minutes late for the meeting. That won't do."

I swallow hard. "Sir, I will do my best to get there on time. There are a few short cuts I can try."

Mr. Kumar smiles. "I'm certain as a Zoomer driver you have acquired quite a roster of alternative routes. Still, it is unfortunate you can't teleport."

It's unlike Mr. Kumar to rub in the fact I still don't have that level of wizarding powers. "I respect the Order's rules. I will put every short cut I know to use."

He chuckles. "I have no doubt, but I fear even with your expertise you will still be late." He places his figure tips together forming a steeple like in the child's game. "Can you keep a secret, Mr. Dunne?"

Suddenly the air in the car feels thick as syrup. My breathing becomes labored. For the second in command to ask me such a thing is beyond monumental. "Of course, sir."

"In the years you have worked for the Order, you have never once asked for a favor." He beams. "Therefore, I am going to transport you to the meeting."

A shiver runs through me. The meeting must be

very important for him to grant such a favor. "Sir, how can I ever thank you?"

I pull over to the side of the road as a blinding light circles my car. Closing my eyes, Mr. Kumar enters my mind. "There is no need. Just do me proud tonight."

❦

MY BEEMER MATERIALIZES INSIDE MY ALLOCATED parking spot in the underground tunnel that runs beneath the Twelfth Order Headquarters.

As I enter the main tunnel of headquarters, the series of leaded glass windows over two stories high still impresses me. They hover above me like giant open wings. They flooded the tunnel with light even though they were coated with what looked like decades of dirt. The walls of the tunnel weren't made of stone like their historic origin as an early subway system would suggest. Instead, they are covered in huge copper metal panels that are riveted together. A series of copper doors stand diagonally across from each other on either side of the tunnel. When I first stood in the main tunnel, I thought it would make the perfect steampunk movie location.

My eyes take in the blinking control consoles that emit a staccato beat as I stand waiting for the meeting to start. It seems there are quite a few operations going on today. Now that I'm early, I get to hang around waiting for my boss to show up. Abject hatred of wasting time is the number one reason I always plan to arrive on time or just five minutes late. My excuse about the LA traffic usually gets a series of eye rolls from my fellow wizards.

I ignore the uniform clad wizards that have formed a group by the main control console. Instead, I walk over to the other side of the tunnel, lean against the copper clad wall, and scroll through my phone to see if I have any ride requests for tonight. My schedule is surprisingly empty. Looks like I might have some time to myself after the meeting. Not that I relish free time since Tara passed. I usually binge watch the latest hot show on Netflix and crash. Unlike what some people might think, we wizards lead boring lives.

The small group of wizards gossiping by the console abruptly stop talking and stand at attention. The powerful scent of roses drifts down the main tunnel signaling someone with extremely powerful magic is moving toward us—the Exemplary Wizard. I brace myself for a snarky comment as he turns the corner and walks past the main control console, ignoring the group of junior wizards. He commands a room as he practically floats across the floor dressed in one of his impeccably tailored Savile Row suits. His blond hair is styled within an inch of its life. The Exemplary Wizard goes against every stereotype you can imagine. No flowing red velvet robes or pointed hat. The long white hair and beards illustrated in storybooks are notably absent as well.

I move behind the group of junior wizards dressed in the standard order issued uniform of brown pants and matching jacket. I'm forever grateful I get to wear nice Kenneth Cole suits instead. My Zoomer assignment does have its advantages. I swallow hard preparing myself for my boss to tease me about arriving early. I've joined the ranks of all the other wizards who love to kiss his ass. At first, he doesn't notice me standing by the large map of Los Angeles's underground tunnels. Then his piercing blue eyes narrow in on me. The hairs on my arms prickle as he continues to stare at me but says nothing. He nods in my direction as if to make a mental note that I for once arrived early.

Then he turns and glides over to greet Mr. Kumar who has miraculously popped out of one of the office rooms that line the main tunnel. The Exemplary Wizard gives Mr. Kumar a knowing smile. "Did you work some kind of magic to get Mr. Dunne here on time?"

I should have known the Exemplary Wizard would suspect such a thing.

The corners of Mr. Kumar's mouth tilt up ever so slightly. "I gave him a bit of encouragement, that is all."

Interesting. Mr. Kumar is powerful enough to lie to his boss. A sign that he will be achieving exemplary status soon.

My boss claps his hands together. "I called this meeting to get updates on the situation with the gas main under Los Angeles City Hall."

Ah. So that is why I'm here. I should have recognized the group of men. Yet, the last time I saw them they were dressed in HAZMAT suits with gas masks and stood fifty feet under Spring Boulevard.

The shortest of the group steps forward. "Sir, the

situation has been remedied thanks to the alert from Mr. Dunne."

Nice to get credit for my reconnaissance work.

He nods in my direction then looks back at the short wizard with a crew cut. "And are you certain your magic will hold? The last thing we need to happen on our watch is for City Hall to explode."

The brunette, who is the tallest of the group, steps forward. "Sir, we arced our powers together to make sure the pipeline will hold."

I bite my lip to keep from laughing as the image from *Ghostbusters* fills my head.

Mr. Kumar turns to his boss. "I double checked their work. It's solid."

The Exemplary Wizard seems unconvinced. "Are you certain it will pass inspection by the gas company?"

Mr. Kumar nods. "Yes, the line looks just as aged and decrepit as it did before."

"Good."

The fact that we wizards of the Twelfth Order go around repairing the dilapidated and dangerous infrastructure of all the major cities in the world still astounds me.

The Exemplary Wizard's eyes narrow in on my slight smile. "Mr. Dunne, is something amusing?"

"No, sir. I'm pleased that everything worked out. Sometimes in the isolation of reconnaissance work you don't know if your emergency notifications truly averted a disaster."

Mr. Kumar strides next to me. "I know you don't

always get to see the results of your tips, but rest assured we keep track of them all."

This was music to my ears. I never had the nerve to ask. I figured if they had a problem with my work, they would have pulled me off Zoomer duty and put me back in the classroom for further training. "Thank you for letting me know, sir."

The Exemplary Wizard waved his hand at the uniformed crew. "Thank you for reporting. That will be all."

My nerves prickle. This wasn't a meeting at all. There is a far more important reason why I have been summoned to headquarters. The Exemplary Wizard gives me a crooked smile that can only mean one thing, he's about to rock my wizard world. "Sir?"

"Mr. Dunne, I have not ignored your ten requests to be given a new assignment."

I try not to act surprised even though I am flabbergasted. For two years I've put in a job transfer form requesting to be taken off my Zoomer reconnaissance assignment like clockwork every two months. I desperately wanted to be assigned something, anything new. All my requests had the same response—silence. "That's wonderful news, sir."

He motions to the trim well-dressed man with salon perfect hair who is lingering by the far end of the control panel. Wait a sec. Where did he come from?

"This is Mr. Pennington. He has a proposition for you."

I give him a warm smile, appreciating his seamless magic. The man gives the Exemplary Wizard a slight bow and then moves next to me. His fruity scented cologne makes my nose twitch.

Between his perfectly manicured fingernails, he holds out a black and white striped business card. "Pleasure to meet you, Mr. Dunne. I'm here to invite you to interview for a position at my division."

I take the card out of his hand and read it. In bold yellow letters framed by striking black cross-hatched shadows it reads, WI-6. Under the large lettering is written, Mr. Pennington—Executive Assistant. I flip the card over and there is an address and time written inside the white stripes. I turn the card back over wondering what the letters mean.

Before I can ask a question, Mr. Pennington says, "I will see you tomorrow at ten sharp."

He turns on his loafer heels and disappears as quickly as he came. The expression on the Exemplary Wizard's face looks like a dog that has devoured something particularly tasty. What has he gotten me into?

A chuckle fills the air. "Mr. Dunne, you are always so amusing."

He read my mind despite my protection spell. Not that I should be surprised. He is the Exemplary Wizard after all. "I try my best, sir. Can I ask, what exactly is WI-6?"

He nods. "You certainly can."

"What do they do at the division? In my five years working for the Twelfth Order, I have never heard anyone mention WI-6 before."

A Cheshire cat grin spreads across his lips. "That's because only a very few wizards even know it exists."

Part of me is flattered by the news, the other is more than a bit apprehensive. "And what exactly do the wizards at WI-6..."

He holds up his hand signaling for me to stop my query. His eyes twinkle like a kid about to open a Christmas present. "It is not my prerogative to tell you."

Fantastic. The division is so secret the Exemplary Wizard himself isn't allowed to mention it. What exactly am I walking into?

"Mr. Dunne. Have no fear." He turns on his gleaming Prada shoes. "All your questions will be answered tomorrow."

INTERVIEW HOT SEAT

I blink hard as I stand in front of a skyscraper I never knew existed until today. I glance at the black and white business card and back at the massive, mirrored tower that gleams in the morning sun. I've been down this block at least ten times in the last month. How could I miss a forty-five-story skyscraper smack dab in the middle of the block? My stomach twists up in knots at the realization I'm standing in another dimension. A portal has been opened for me. The WI-6 wields a power I could never imagine. All the magic I've seen performed by the Twelfth Order is extraordinary, yet this kind of power makes me queasy. Part of me hopes I flunk the interview. The Exemplary Wizard is no picnic, but he is appreciative of my quirky ways. WI-6 reeks of power. They surely must be a strictly business division. How else could they exist without anyone but a select few wizards knowing?

The timer on my watch buzzes reminding me I

have five minutes to make my way to the interview. Despite an underlying feeling of dread, I take several large strides forward and enter the building through its massive mirror clad doors.

My apprehension subsides a bit when I see that the lobby is typical of many skyscrapers in Los Angeles. The black marble lobby is empty except for one guard standing next to a large back of black-mirrored elevators. A pretty blonde in her mid-thirties sits behind a black-mirrored desk. I walk up to her trying to ooze confidence even though I don't have any. "I have a ten o'clock appointment with Mr. Bullock."

She looks me up and down hopefully approving of my tailored black suit accented by a subtle deep navy and eggplant striped tie. She nods and reaches out to hand me a badge and a key card. "Place the badge over your jacket pocket. Use the key card to access the elevator. Mr. Bullock's office is on the forty-fifth floor." She pauses and then flashes me a smile. "Nice tie."

I return her a smile with one of my own and place the badge on top of my jacket. It miraculously sticks to it as if I have a huge magnet in my pocket. The WI-6 use some smooth magic. With only two minutes left, I put the card key in the illuminated slot and the elevator doors slide open. As I step inside, the doors close in less than a blink of an eye. With the force of a space rocket, I am propelled up to the forty-fifth floor in less than thirty seconds. I can see why other paranormals complain that wizards are a bunch of showoffs. The WI-6 wizards seem to not shy away from displaying their skills.

The doors silently glide open, and another gleaming empty space greets me. I'm beginning to wonder if there is anyone else in the building. Could they have created the skyscraper to impress me? I admit so far it is working.

From around the corner a familiar face appears. It's Mr. Pennington, Mr. Bullock's somewhat eccentric assistant. He could give Mr. Kumar some competition for most flamboyant dresser. Scott is wearing a bright lavender suit with a pale turquoise tie. He greets me with a quick smile and an outstretch hand. "Mr. Dunne."

I shake his hand firmly. "Your headquarters is quite impressive. I've never noticed it on Spring Street before."

His smile holds firm. "I'm sure it must be red Corvette syndrome."

"Sir?"

He laughs. "One day you see a red Corvette drive up next to your car and think I've never seen one before. Then the rest of the week all you notice are red Corvettes."

I nod feeling stupid that I didn't get the analogy right off the bat. "Sorry, I'm a bit off my game."

Scott reaches over and pats my shoulder. "It is all right. But please don't be nervous about the interview." He leans in closer. "Between you and me, it is really just a formality. When we are out of ear shot of my boss, please call me Scott."

He motions for me to follow him as he moves down the hall into the forty-fifths floor lobby. "The meeting is just a formality", lingers in my brain. How can that be? Did I make that good of an impression on Scott at our first meeting? No, it can't be that. Before I can ponder the question any further, Scott opens the walnut door to Mr. Bullock's office. I try not to act like a kid in a candy store as I take in the sleek futuristic technology displayed on the back console of the office. Yet, despite the electronic eye candy, a large walnut desk takes center stage. My eyes move over to the multiple screens covering one wall and a bank of blinking lights to rival the ones at the Twelfth Order Headquarters. I'm faced by a mind-blowing view. The heart of downtown Los Angeles appears to be floating around us in a bank of clouds. I swallow hard realizing I am standing inside a powerful wizard's creation. In this case the air is not filled with the smell of roses, but that of peonies. Maybe each branch of upper echelon wizards has their own particular scent to signify their power. In a way it makes sense. That way other wizard orders can recognize each other.

As I look back toward the center of the room, the sleek walnut desk now has someone sitting behind it. Talk about making an appearance. Mr. Bullock is a big man by the look of the upper part of his body. There is something distinctly Italian about his facial features. His heritage seems odd with a name like Mr. Bullock. He sits clad in an impeccably tailored black pin-striped suit with a Gucci logo tie. "So, you are the Mr. Dunne I have heard so much about."

He flicks his wrist, and a black leather chair materializes in front of the desk. If I weren't a wizard myself, I'd think I was in the middle of a magician's act.

I sit down in the chair and try to act relaxed. There is something very sharp and pointed about Mr. Bullock's face that reminds me of a shark. My instincts tell me if he smells a bit of weakness, I'm not getting the job. "Yes, sir. Derrick Dunne to be precise."

There is a twinkle in his eyes. "I heard you are a bit cheeky."

Interesting. A British term but Mr. Bullock has a decidedly American accent. "Sir. I'm known for speaking my mind. Is that a problem?"

The corners of his mouth turn up. "Not at all. I informed your superior I was looking for a wizard who possessed confidence. You seem to fit the bill nicely. What other attributes would you say you possess?"

The standard employer question that usually gets people in trouble. As I look into Mr. Bullock's almost black eyes, I have no fear of screwing up the interview. I can always go back to my Zoomer job. Leaning back in the chair, I smile at him like we are old friends. "I am told I'm an out of the box thinker."

Mr. Bullock nods and strokes his tiny mustache. "That is an attribute in our line of work to be sure. Give me an example of one of your more creative solutions to a problem that you have encountered."

A smile spreads across my face when I think fondly of Fred, who just happens to be my friend Brooklyn's bat familiar. "I had an emergency call that there was going to be an attack on what was then called the

Staples Center, which is now known as Crypto.com Center."

Scott bursts out laughing. "Isn't that the worst sell-out merch name you've ever heard? At least Staples Center had a ring to it."

Mr. Burrow's forehead crinkles, then he gives his assistant the evil eye. With his message delivered Mr. Bullock turns back to me. "As you were saying, Mr. Dunne." Then he holds up one of his fingers. "For clarification. I believe your current job is as a reconnaissance and first responder Twelfth Order wizard. Is that correct?"

I nod, never hearing my complex job boiled down to so few words. "Yes, sir. On the day I received the threat to the Staples Center, I had to do some quick thinking. Not knowing whether the enemy was an ordinary person who hates the world, a wizard, or another paranormal gone bad. I felt using magic would be ill advised."

Mr. Bullock leans forward placing his elbows on the walnut desk. "Was this a gut reaction, or did you have a tip?"

"My gut, sir." I rubbed my washboard stomach from hours of doing sit ups while waiting for Zoomer customers or a catastrophe that could destroy Los Angeles. "I'm fortunate it has good instincts."

Mr. Pennington stifles a laugh before Mr. Bullock could give him a disapproving glare. "The detectives of WI-6 rely on their gut as well."

Fantastic. I finally find out what the wizards of WI-6 do for a living. Now I really want the job. I've been a

Sherlock Holmes fanatic since junior high school. "I wouldn't be alive today without my instincts."

He nods and his elbows creep forward another inch. "Continue."

"I wracked my brain for how I could quickly find out where the bomb had been placed at the center. Then I thought of Fred."

The suspense of my tale had Scott on the edge of his seat. "Was he some kind of paranormal that can see through walls?"

I shook my head. "Not exactly. Fred is the bat familiar to my witch friend Brooklyn. I used his sonar ability to track down the bomber and the location of the device he was about to detonate."

Mr. Bullock cracks a smile. "Very clever. Just curious, but was the bomber one of us?" "No, sir, it was your standard issue psychopath. But I had to make a snap decision."

Mr. Bullock sat back in his cushy executive leather chair. "Being cautious is very important to a detective's job. The Exemplarily Wizard said you have been seeking a job transfer for several years. You seem quite well adapted to your reconnaissance work. Why did you want to transfer?"

"I like being challenged when I work. Not that reconnaissance doesn't keep me on my toes. There is constantly something new—but..."

"Anything can become boring after a few years."

I'm starting to like Mr. Bullock. "Yes. I am not the type of wizard who likes things easy."

He smiles and touches his mustache. "Yes. The

Exemplary Wizard warned me about your tendency to make things difficult for yourself."

I wonder what other tidbits he told him. Not enough to scare Mr. Bullock off of wanting to interview me. "It's true. Sometimes I do myself no favors. But I like to think I always come through in the end."

Mr. Bullock snaps his fingers and a small viewing screen hovers in front of him. "From what I can see on your employment records I procured from the Twelfth Order head of WR, you have only been written up a few times early in your wizarding career. I don't see anything for the last several years."

"I like to think I have matured on the job."

Mr. Bullock nods, snaps his fingers and the viewing screen disappears. "I'd like Scott to show you around the place. Congratulations, you've made it through the first round."

In the time it takes me to stand up, Mr. Bullock has vanished. I turn to Scott. "Does he always do that?"

He chuckles. "My boss loves to make a dramatic entrance and exit."

"He sure does. I must say I'm a bit surprised he did the first phase of the interview. It seems Mr. Bullock would have the last say."

Scott snickers. "Oh, he does, trust me." He holds out his arm and directs me toward a barely visible door. "Let me show you what we detectives lovingly call, *The Pit*."

Terrific. And just when I thought things were going so well. "Lead the way."

With a snap of Scott finger the door becomes

three-dimensional and pops open. The WI-6 wizard's magic is flawless. If I get hired, I am going to have to up my spell game.

The name of *The Pit* becomes obvious when we enter a vast space so dimly lit, I can hardly see where I'm going. I run into a desk and rub my leg.

Scott chuckles. "Sorry, I should have warned you to cast a visibility spell before we entered the room."

I nod and cast the spell and instantly the dark void becomes brighter. The room is still quite dark, but at least now I can see the outlines of two rows of desks and the faint outlines of the men and women behind them.

A woman with long auburn hair gets up and greets me. In a sultry deep voice she says, "Hello, Mr. Dunne. Welcome to *The Pit*. This is the home base for the investigative team of WI-6. If you pass the interview, you will be working here."

I smile thinking how *The Pit* is not much different than working in the tunnels under Los Angeles. "Is there a reason for the dim lighting? Are the detectives part mole?"

A pleasant laugh escapes her dark red lips. "I can't wait to tell the guys what you said. I've teased them many times about being like rodents."

Scott waves me over to the woman. "Ms. Burke will take it from here. I'll see you back in the lobby when you are through."

Before I can thank Scott, he disappears with the same seamless skill of his boss. Disappearing seems to be a trademark of the WI-6 wizards.

Ms. Burke loops her arm around mine. "You'll find we aren't nearly as stuffy as the boys who work under Mr. Bullock."

Ms. Burke seems to be taking me under her wing. Or maybe it's all an act. My gut seems to be taking a vacation, as it has no reaction to Ms. Burke one-way or the other.

She leads me over to a desk that is separate from the two rows. A large desk lords over The Pit from the back of the room.

A bald man who barely clears the top of his desk busily taps away at a keyboard.

Ms. Burke clears her throat. "Mr. Pierre, Mr. Dunne is ready for you."

His head darts up and I bite my lip. Mr. Pierre looks like the spitting image of Monsieur Hercule Poirot from the Agatha Christie novels. I bite my lip to keep from laughing.

His small, dark eyes, scan my face. In a classic French accent he says, "Mr. Dunne," He waves a short arm toward a chair that pops up out of the floor. "Have a seat."

I sit down in the most uncomfortable plastic patio chair I've ever sat on. This guy means to set me off my game. As I try to settle into the firm seat of the chair, I know he is winning.

Mr. Pierre looks over at a viewing screen that hovers next to the keyboard. "Mr. Dunne, your recommendations from Mr. Kumar and the Exemplary Wizard are quite impressive."

I let out a tiny gasp at the realization that the

Exemplary Wizard cared enough about me to write a recommendation. "Thank you, sir."

His dark eyes narrow in on mine. "You seem surprised to receive a recommendation for the Exemplary Wizard. You shouldn't be. Your record is exemplary."

His word choice is not lost on me. "In my line of work, you are constantly putting out fires. You don't really have time to look back on what you have accomplished."

He nods. "I can see how that would be true. Here at WI-6 we have a similar pace. But I do my best to rotate my detectives, so they do not reach the burn out point as I am afraid you have, Mr. Dunne."

It seems Mr. Pierre snuck in a little mind reading before I sat down. Or maybe my burn out is written all over my face. "I admit that is the reason I am here looking for another line of work. I must say I am surprised to be considered for WI-6. I have no background in sleuthing."

Mr. Pierre strokes his mustache and chuckles. His round belly punctuates each laugh at my expense. "But you are wrong, Mr. Dunne. You have proved yourself to be quite an instinctive detective. Your work history proves it. Such natural ability is rather rare."

Could that be the reason I'm here? "Thank you, sir but I was just doing my job."

He leans back in his chair with a quizzical look on his face. "I hear you are quite witty. Tell me a wizard joke."

He must be kidding. "Sir, is this question a joke?"

He twirls the left side of his mustache and forms it into the shape of a J. "No, it is not."

This is the strangest job interview. Like something out of a bad movie. "All right. Why did two wizards show up to a battle empty handed?"

"I have no idea."

"Because they left their weapons at a staff meeting."

The laugh erupted out of his belly like a volcano.

Ms. Burke races over to Mr. Pierre as he struggles for air. "Sir, are you alright? Did Mr. Dunne say something to upset you?" She snaps her fingers and holds out a large crystal glass filled with water. "Here, sir. Please drink this down."

He waves the glass away and sputters out, "I'm fine, Miss Burke. "He took a deep breath. "Truly fine."

She glares at me, and I realize I need to apologize. "I'm sorry, sir. I know it is a stupid joke, but it was quite popular back at Twelfth Order Headquarters."

He smiles and straightens his mustache. "I'm certain it was. Quite clever."

If someone asked me when I thought I landed the job as WI-6 detective, they would never believe it was after telling a bad wizard joke.

Once Mr. Pierre regains his composure, he snaps his fingers, and a viewing screen materializes before me. "One final question. Based on the appearance of the three men and one woman on the screen, which one do you think is a murderer. You are not allowed to use any magic to answer the question."

Talk about going from laughs to the fire. My confidence deflated like a balloon. In school I was always terrible at guessing answers to tests. I took in the prospective murderers knowing they couldn't be more different from each other. The first man was short and stout like Mr. Pierre, and he even sported the same mustache. Yet, he couldn't be dressed more differently. Instead of an impeccable suit, the man wore a pale blue polo shirt and plaid shorts. I couldn't help noticing his legs had so much dark hair his pale skin was hardly visible. Man number two, sported a halo of ginger locks that accented his round face. He wore a plaid button-down shirt and khaki trousers. The third suspect turned out to be a woman. She had the girl-next-door looks of Jennifer Aniston. Yet, she wore a black T-shirt that said "Make My Day" in bold red letters, topped off by a pair of strategically torn faded jeans. Last on the possible killer list stood the final man. He resembled Charles Manson on a good day. His eyes had the same crazy stare. One that felt like it looked right through you. He wore an impeccably tailored pin-striped suit the Exemplary Wizard would be proud to hang in his closet. To say the candidates are sending mixed messages is an understatement of epic proportions. Ms. Burke beams as she takes in my crinkled-up forehead. "No one promised round two of the interview would be a breeze."

My eyes drift over to the chair behind the huge desk that Mr. Pierre no longer occupies. Had I disappointed him so much he felt the need to vanish? "Where has your boss disappeared too?"

She shrugs her shoulders. "He tends to vanish when

we are in the middle of something. We're used to it around here."

Well at least it wasn't because of me. I better kiss up to Ms. Burke as she now has complete control of my interview. Sensing she played a part in how the prospective murderers were dressed, I decide to give her a compliment. "The mixed messaging in the possible killers' wardrobes was quite impressive."

Her red lips part, revealing a perfect celebrity smile. "Thanks." Then she glances at her watch. "Time is up. Which one is the killer?"

My eyes cruise over the photos on the viewing screen one more time. "I like how you dressed the Jennifer Aniston look-alike as her evil twin."

Ms. Burke's eyes grow wide. "Is that your choice?"

I sit back in my chair thinking her reaction means the girl is not the murderer. "The Charles Manson in a business suit is quite the mash-up as well."

Her smile vanishes. "Quit stalling. You have two seconds to give me your answer."

My gut chooses two candidates. The girl and the Hercule Poirot, aka Mr. Pierre's, clone. Throwing in a choice so closely resembling my possible future boss smacks of some kind of test. "I pick number one. Anyone with legs that hairy has to be a murderer."

Ms. Burke doesn't even crack a smile. "Your answer is duly noted." Her gaze drifts over to a spot in the left corner of the dark space of *The Pit* and then back to me. Someone has been watching my interview, more than likely Mr. Bullock.

Ms. Burke motions for me to get up. I follow her back to the main door of *The Pit*.

She flings it open and says, "Tomorrow you should receive a text from Mr. Pennington if you are going to join our team."

I assume silence if I didn't live up to WI-6's standards. I hesitate in the doorway for a moment longer. Maybe I can still win some points. "It was a pleasure meeting you, Ms. Burke." I flash her my best, *I'm a nice guy please hire me* smile. "I hope to see you again soon."

My charm offensive seems to have worked as she graces me with a red lip framed smile. "We shall see."

3

———

LIMBO

Climbing into my Beemer, I can feel a major after interview hangover coming on. I suddenly wished I can take the day off. A strange limbo hangs over me like a storm cloud. I have no idea if this was my last day of working reconnaissance for the Twelfth Order or just another day of many trying to save Los Angeles from itself.

Before I can turn off of Spring Street onto Hill Street to the Twelfth Order Headquarters, a text pops up on my screen.

"I'm sure the last thing you want to deal with today is an emergency call, but fate is sometimes not kind."

Typical Mr. Kumar. He is a realist to the core. "An incident was reported out in Larchmont. Sending you the coordinates now."

Well, at least I won't have time to dwell on how the interview went. I turn the wheel hard and head toward the trendy older part of Los Angeles. As I scan my GPS to find the shortest route my phone buzzes through. "Hey, Der. Can you give me a ride in twenty?"

Krissy at her demanding best. "Sorry, I have another gig."

She purrs through the phone. "Who is she?"

Werewolves and their propensity to jealousy. "It isn't a she... I have a job interview." A little white lie about the timing but mostly the truth.

She sighs. "I'm so tired of wizards playing hard to get."

The phone clicks off and I'm left to ponder what other wizards Krissy might know. My ego is a bit bruised knowing I'm not the only wizard she has lusted after. Yet, I can't help cracking a smile that I'm the only one to deny her.

A new message flashes on the screen from Mr. Kumar. "I was remiss in not sending you the background on the Larchmont event. Last week one of the C team members spotted some suspicious activity near a long ago sealed off aqueduct. There was an old entrance near the golf course at the Wilshire Country Club. The exit point is now buried under a restaurant on North Larchmont Boulevard. I need you to figure out what exactly is some evil person's plan. I know it's a lot for your possible last day with us. But I thought I should send our or best wizard."

Mr. Kumar clicks off and I'm not focused on what could become quite the complicated mission but, on his words, *"possible last day."* Could he have heard something from Mr. Bullock? No, I would think he would want to tell the Exemplary Wizard, himself not his second in command.

I shook my head knowing I needed to focus my brain power on whatever might be afoot in Larchmont. As I drive down Fairfax, I used a spell to block my phone from incoming calls. The last thing I need is to have a Zoomer call come in while I'm doing reconnaissance.

The address Mr. Kumar gave me leads me to a cute little restaurant called Wick & Scones. I love the play on words. I park my car and realize wearing a fancy suit is going to make me stand out and not in a good way. I snap my fingers, and in the suits place, are a pair of black trousers and a grey and black striped shirt. It's my go to outfit when I'm trying to blend in with a crowd composed of business casual and trendy Westsiders. Then I climb out of the car click the lock and put my debit card in the meter and wince when I see how much an hour costs. The Westside of Los Angeles is notorious for its exorbitant parking fees. Knowing the place in question is a restaurant makes my entrance to the back of the space easy. Meet Derrick Dunne, health inspector. I snap my fingers and an official Los Angeles health department ID materializes on a lanyard around my neck. I peer into the window and only see a few people gathered at two tables.

I stride through the door with the confidence I assume a health inspector possesses. I walk up to the counter and look up at the menu, appreciative of more word play in the names of the sconces. Blueberry bungler, raspberry Katy Perry. The wick part of the name assaults my senses as at least ten candles are burning with various floral scents completely overpowering the aroma of fresh baked goods. The word play of Wick & Scones is clever, but the actual reality of candles and scones together is another story. Yet, the few people sitting chatting while drinking tea and eating their sconces seem not to be bothered by the candle fragrances dominating the restaurant.

A cute young girl with the restaurant T-shirt asks, "What can I get you? The raspberry Katy Perry are fresh out of the oven."

"That sounds delicious but I'm here for another reason." I hold out my health inspector ID and she winces.

She holds up a finger. "Wait one sec. Let me get Shawn. He's the manager."

I move away from the counter when the doorbell rings and a guy dressed in what could be considered a Westside uniform of lavender shirt with black denim jeans strolls up to the counter. I hide my ID not wanting to cause a problem for the owner.

A tall thin man about thirty with platinum dyed hair appears from a side door. The young guy waves. "Hey, Shawn, how's it going?"

Shawn gives me the stink eye. "Great." He points to the girl behind the counter. "Get Bran whatever he wants." He smiles at Bran. "It's on me."

Bran excitedly runs over to the counter as if Shawn just announced he won the bakery lottery.

Shawn motions for me to follow him through a swing door that leads to the kitchen. His eyes grow wide. "Are you here because of a complaint by Marsha Tull? I swear she put her own hair in the clotted cream. The baker and his workers all wear hair nets, and no one has purple hair. We run a clean kitchen here."

As I eye the gleaming tan linoleum floor and the spotless baking ovens, their stainless steel polished to mirror like perfection, I can understand why he is so upset. "I can't divulge the name of the person who complained. I'm here to inspect the kitchen and write a report." I give Shawn and easy smile. "But by the looks of things, you have nothing to worry about."

Shawn taps on a door to the left of where I am standing. A guy wearing a ridiculously high chef's hat and sporting a silly mustache like Mr. Pierre's races over to the top oven. "You are going to have to inspect around me. I must tend to the ovens. Scones are very particular about their baking time."

I nod like I understand and pull out a small palm sized computer like the one's restaurant server's use. "No problem. I'll get my report done as quickly as possible but as soon as you check the ovens, I need to be alone in the kitchen."

The baker crinkles up his nose, causing his pencil thin mustache to twitch. "I have two ovens worth of scones that need tending."

"As I said, I'll complete my report as quickly as possible."

With a loud huff and a smash of his wrist on the swinging door, the baker disappears. Shawn shrugs and follows behind him.

I cast a visibility spell and search for a sign of the

old aqueduct opening. The spell makes me feel like Superman every time I use it. At first, I find nothing. Then I spy a section of the wall next to the ovens that doesn't look right. I run my hand along the edge and can tell there is something behind the wall. My instincts tell me there is an access point, but I can't explore it now. I'll have the Order transport me inside. In the meantime, I need to make sure I don't blow my cover.

I bang a few bowls around and look around the industrial sized dough mixer. The baker is meticulous. Not a spec of flour or sugar anywhere. Knowing what little I do about baking, this level of cleanliness must be done by magic. That explains how the baker can keep the kitchen running smoothly and work in the aqueduct tunnel at the same time. A shiver runs down my spine. Is he a wizard gone bad? Can he sense what I am? I better get out of here just in case he is suspicious. I smear a bit of grease on my shirt from a baking sheet and push on the swing door. "I'm all done!"

A collective sigh comes from the baker and Shawn. The baker races back into the kitchen while Shawn approaches me with a forced smile. "So how did we do?"

"I'm not supposed to tell you anything. A copy of the report will be emailed to you as soon as it's processed."

Shawn holds out a scone. "Something for the road."

"I'm not supposed to take bribes either." I gingerly grab the scone and take a bite. It's delicious. The blueberries explode in my mouth. I wipe the juice from my lower lip. "I don't think you have anything to worry about in my report. Thanks for the scone."

Shawn is so excited he races over with a candle gift box. "Thank you so much."

I take the box from him and smile. "I won't say anything about the bribes if you don't tell my boss I tipped you off on the report."

Shawn beams. "Deal." He holds the door open for me. "Come back anytime."

I nod, knowing I'm not truly leaving. "I will."

Thanks to a quick text and the powers of the Twelfth Order transporter machine, I'm standing behind the wall of the Wick & Scone's kitchen. My reconnaissance starts in earnest. Using the flashlight on my phone I make my way down an old tunnel long forgotten until the wizard disguised as a baker decides to open it back up. Now I just need to figure out what he is up to.

At first, I see nothing that would cause me alarm but as I work my way further down the tunnel, an acrid odor burns my nostrils. I quickly conjure a fume mask to protect myself. The faint sound of running water grows louder as I continue down the tunnel. The stonewalls are the obvious remnants of the old aqueduct system that used to bring water to the area long before it was Los Angeles.

I literally stumble upon several metal containers with skull and cross bones danger labels plastered on the front. I hold my phone over the label to read what is inside the container. The hair on the back of my neck bristles when I see in bold black letters the words

Cyanide Chloride. The wizard is going to poison the water at the Wilshire Country Club as a test. At first it seems a strange move, until I realize that the crowd that hangs out at the club and plays golf there are some of the most powerful people in the Los Angeles business world. The turmoil a mass poisoning would cause in the Los Angeles elite would be felt way outside the city. Now I realize why Mr. Kumar flagged this as an emergency. I text headquarters to stage a bomb scare at the country club to clear everyone out. Then I need to decide what I'm going to do about the wizard gone bad.

CLOSING MY EYES, I USE A HOMING SPELL TO RETURN to my car. I tap the screen and contact Mr. Kumar. "I checked and the wizard is still inside the Wick & Scone. You need to send a team to get him out of there. He's already seen me."

The distinctive British Indian accent fills my car. "I will send team D to deal with him."

"Do you know who the renegade wizard is?"

"Yes, unfortunately. He is a defector from Severance."

I purse my lips. Severance is a powerful organization in its own right. Unfortunately for their command, a percentage of the wizards in training tend to be malcontents. I always think of them like medieval knights that turn traitor and fight for a rival king. They used to be loyal warriors and then decided to go off on their own, throwing their honor away like rotten fruit.

"Has the Order done anything to help stem the flow at Severance? This must be the fourth wizard to defect this year."

Mr. Kumar sighs. "Their commanding wizard keeps promising to resolve the situation, but it may come to shutting them down."

Something unthinkable in the wizard world. "I hope things don't come to that. I remember in my wizarding history class that the last clash became quite violent. Spells have only grown more powerful since then."

"I do too. It's been many centuries since we have had to close a branch. None in my lifetime." There is a moment of silence at the significance of his words. Mr. Kumar is over a hundred and fifty years old. "Good job, Mr. Dunne. A pleasure working with you."

Is he teasing me yet again? Although even if he is, it's nice to have Mr. Kumar in my corner for getting the detective job. I wonder if the Exemplary Wizard has heard from Mr. Bullock yet. Mr. Kumar clicks off and I lean back in my seat exhausted. I close my eyes and wait for backup. When I open my eyes again, I smile as I see team D has arrived on the scene. I'm grateful they are the cleanup crew, not me. I turn on the engine of my Beemer wanting nothing more than to head back to my apartment and crash. Believe it or not wizards have to sleep every once in a while.

I make the turn onto Beverly Boulevard forcing my eyes to stay open, so I don't crash the car and then my phone rings. The last thing I need is to be sidetracked from my bed. I sure hope it's not Mr. Kumar wanting me to report into headquarters. "I need a ride from Panache restaurant in Melrose to the Beverly Hilton Hotel. Are you available?"

Not the British Indian voice I expected. A decidedly female one. How did her call make it through my spell? I don't remember setting a time limit. I sigh and click on the line. "I'm actually going to close out my rides for today. I can refer you to another reliable Zoomer driver."

There is a tinge of disappointment in her melodic voice. "It is a short drive. Less than fifteen minutes, I believe. I'll be waiting in front of Panache. Are you certain you can't do one last trip?"

In case by some crazy twist of fate this woman is related to Mr. Kumar, I decide I better pick her up. "Okay. I'll be there in ten."

I speed along La Brea heading up to trendy Melrose. Part of me wishes I could only be reached through the real Zoomer app so I could have pre-screened her request. But I must face the fact that my number has been circulating throughout the LA paranormal world since I first started driving. I wonder who gave this woman my number? I've learned not everyone is paranormal who uses my service. Sometimes the Order likes to cycle through regular people to keep me on my toes. I wonder which one this woman is.

I turn down Melrose looking for the restaurant Panache. Not that it is hard to miss with its bright purple painted brick façade. I stop in front of the restaurant next to a strikingly beautiful woman. Her good looks are similar to Mr. Kumar's handsomeness.

She could easily be another candidate for the Bollywood screen. Her red cocktail dress is just the right amount of tight and sexy. She nods when she sees me pull up next to her. I put the car in park and get out to open the door for her. She smiles and tucks into the back seat. "Thank you. It's nice to know there are still drivers that are gentlemen."

I stride toward the driver's door, appreciative of the compliment. Some paranormals like Krissy take my politeness for granted. I'm tempted to ask her how she got my number but decide against it. Instead, I lean back, enjoying the wonderful scent of her perfume as it drifts toward me. It's vaguely familiar, something I enjoyed on a woman in the past, but the name of the woman and the perfume escapes me. "That is a lovely fragrance you are wearing."

She looks up from her phone. "Ah, it's a personal favorite but a bit old fashioned. It's called Shalimar."

I nod in recognition. "A classic to be sure. It has a nice mix of exotic fragrances."

She lets out a light laugh. "It suits my personality."

I can't help but think it also matches her looks, but I say nothing. Women like her get complimented on their beauty every day. The one thing I've learned from Krissy is that being desired can be a chore. I decide to change the subject to safer territory. "How do you like the Beverly Hilton?"

Her perfectly arched brows move upward. "It's an older hotel, but I enjoy the classics."

I give her a smile. "Who doesn't love a classic?" Not only is she stunning, but I could also appreciate her dry wit. "Are you visiting Los Angeles for the first time?"

She turns and looks out the window. "My first time for work. I came once before when I was younger. We went to all the amusement parks. It was my sixteenth birthday present."

"Wow, that was quite the gift. You were a lucky girl."

She laughs and the car is filled with a wondrous sound, like bird song. "I was the only girl in my family of six, so my father spoiled me terribly. My brothers never let me forget how jealous they were. They had to stay home with my mother."

"Ouch. Did you rub it in by showing them endless pictures and videos when you came home?"

Her eyes grow large. "How did you know?"

"Because I had a spoiled rotten kid sister too. You girls are flat out evil."

Her musical laugh fills the car again. There was an ease in our conversation that surprised me. It feels like I've known her far longer than ten minutes.

She stops laughing. "I do understand your pain, truly."

As I pull up to the front of the Beverly Hilton, I feel a pang of sadness that I more than likely won't see this wonderful woman again. The price of being a Zoomer driver. As I move past the front of the hotel, I admire the perfectly manicured flower beds filled with begonias and boxwood. The beds frame a large circular fountain that bubbles away ignoring my melancholy. I pull into the circular drive and the woman places a hundred-dollar bill on the center console. "Thank you for giving me a lift."

As I take the bill from the console my hand brushes hers. Heat radiates up my arm. I haven't felt this attracted to a woman since the day I first met Tara. I glance back down at the hundred-dollar bill. It is quite the exorbitant tip considering she already paid the fair by tapping her credit card. "Are you sure?"

She nods. "It's my way of thanking you for a pleasant ride and for going out of your way."

As the doorman reaches over to open her door, I can't help but wish I could see her again. "If you need a ride while you are here, it would be my pleasure to take you around Los Angeles."

As she eases out of the car, she flashes me a final smile. "I'll be sure to keep that in mind."

The red of her dress disappears behind a group of businessmen getting ready to take on the night life of Los Angeles. I take in one last flash of her shiny, long dark hair, and then she vanishes inside the hotel. I'm a bit surprised by how much I want to see her again. All I can do is hope that fate will bring us together again.

4

DOG GONE

I wake up at my usual time, six o'clock, and eye the sun streaming through the crack in the bedroom drapes—my natural alarm clock. My hopes of getting a clue of my job situation are still answered by silence. Even though the power of WI-6 is a bit intimidating, I get a thrill when I think about the possibility of working as a detective. The thought is soon squashed by a viewing screen materializing at the foot of my bed. The usual Twelfth Order morning briefing is starting. Mr. Kumar fills in the members on our aqueduct discovery. He posts a picture of the wizard who posed as a baker. As I know the story well, and sleep evaded me most of the night, it takes mere seconds for my eyes to flutter shut.

A commanding voice startles me awake. My eyes flutter open to find the Exemplary Wizard staring back at me. Instead of getting chastised for sleeping through the briefing, he greets me with laughter. "Are our morning briefings so dreary they induce sleep?"

I push up onto my pillows and I'm soon sitting ramrod straight. "No, sir, not at all. I did not sleep well last night."

His smile seems to be mocking me. "Could the reason for your lack of sleep be from staying up all night celebrating your wizard gone bad discovery? Or could it be from wondering how your interview went?"

"The latter, sir."

"Well, I will hold you in suspense no longer. I received a call from Mr. Bullock bright and early this morning."

I sit patiently, waiting for the news of my fate. Knowing the Exemplary Wizard all too well, I know he is going to string this out for a while. One of his particularly irritating qualities. "That is interesting. And what did you talk about?'

True to his character he says, "A bit of this and that."

"Anything in regard to me, sir?"

His smile fades. "Yes, at the end of our conversation."

He doesn't need to say more. Looks like I'll be a Zoomer driver for good. "If that is all, sir. I need to get ready for work."

His smile returns. "You do indeed."

"Does Mr. Kumar have a new assignment for me?"

The Exemplary Wizard's brow furrows. "No."

I toss my legs over the side of my bed. "Then I better get ready for my Zoomer clients."

The Exemplary Wizard clears his throat. "I understand you are sleep deprived so you may be a bit daft."

Oh, oh. The Exemplary Wizard never insults his employees unless we crossed a major line. "I'm sorry, sir. I admit I'm not at my sharpest this morning."

He nods. "That is for certain. The job I was referring to is the one you will be starting today at WI-6."

GAZING UP AT THE SKYSCRAPER ON SPRING STREET, I realize I haven't had many dreams become true moments in my life. In fact, I've only had two others. The day a scout from the Twelfth Order approached my father about my joining the Order and the moment Tara looked me in the eyes and told me she loved me. Somehow it felt fitting that a new opportunity came along now. I was lost and confused about my new adult life when the Order scout found me. Likewise, when Tara entered my life, I thought I would be a bachelor forever. She proved me wrong. As I walk toward the entrance to WI-6 I know this is another pivotal moment in my life. I could feel it in my bones.

Scott greets me in the lobby wearing a pale green suit. I wonder if he buys his clothes in Miami, they are so colorful.

He holds out his hand. "Welcome to WI-6, Mr. Dunne. Didn't I predict you had the interview in the bag?"

I laugh as I shake his hand. "You did. Please, call me Derrick."

He nods and moves to the elevators. "Like I said when we first meet, when we are alone together it would be a pleasure to be on a first name basis." He pulls a keycard out of his jacket pocket. "However, we're kind of formal here, so it's company policy to call everyone by their surname."

I nod and take the keycard with my name and photo on it. I suddenly feel very official. "Understood, Mr. Pennington."

He chuckles. "I hope you ate a good breakfast, because we have quite the action-packed day planned for you. First, we need to take you to Wizard Resources to fill out some paperwork. Then I'll introduce you to the rest of the detectives at The Pit. We will close out the day with a meeting with Mr. Bullock."

"That is action packed. Too bad I just had a cup of coffee for breakfast."

He gives me a knowing smile. "The breakfast of champions." The elevator doors slide open, and we walk inside. Scott pushes the button and leans against the wall of the elevator. "Don't worry. I'll be sure we squeeze in at least a half hour for lunch." He reaches into his jacket pocket again and pulls out a protein bar. "Here. Hopefully this will tide you over. I have a stash in my desk. Be forewarned you should do the same. Time for a relaxing lunch is almost nonexistent here."

My instincts about WI-6 being strictly business were right. "Thanks for the heads up. I'll be sure to stop by Traders and grab a couple of boxes of my favorite protein bars."

We rocket to the thirtieth floor. I follow Scoot

down a brightly illuminated hallway with doors on either side. He stops in front of door number six that is labeled in gold eight-inch letters, Wizard Resources.

He taps me on the shoulder. "I'll be back to get you in an hour."

"Filling out a few forms takes that long?"

Scott chuckles. "The forms take fifteen minutes. It's the instructional video that takes most of the time."

I give him a smile having watched my share of Twelfth Order instructional videos. "I'm sure I'm in for a treat."

Scott's laughter echoes down the hallway as he heads back to the elevator. I suck in a deep calming breath and enter the Wizard Resource office. Instead of being greeted by a sterile room, my eyes are dazzled by an enormous mural that takes up the entire back wall of the office. Life sized colorful parrots fly in a cloudless blue sky over a tropical paradise. If the object of the mural is to put me at ease and make me want to book a vacation to Costa Rica, it's working.

My ease quickly vanishes when a woman dressed in a black pantsuit with hair to match greets me with an expressionless face. Her hair is pulled tightly into a severe bun at the back of her neck. "Mr. Dunne, follow me."

Her high-heeled boots clack on the hardwood floor as she leads me down a hallway lined with offices. She opens the door at the end of the hallway, and I am greeted by a stunning view of the central library. She motions to the single chair in front of a glass desk. "I'd like to go over a few things before you sign the contract."

"Yes, of course." I sit down in a black leather director type chair designed only for looks.

She leans back in her plush executive leather chair. "We run a tight ship here at WI-6. Mr. Bullock is first and foremost a businessman. That is why he was chosen to be the new head of the division two years ago. He runs the division like a fortune five hundred company. There has been quite the turnaround since he took over."

I try not to slump in my chair at the news. My guess about the division was right on the money. "Understood."

Her dark eyes narrow in on mine. "I thought I should give you fair warning, as I hear the Twelfth Order is run like a frat house."

I press my lips together to keep from laughing. The Exemplary Wizard would be infuriated at the comparison and more than likely turn whoever started the rumor into a crab with no legs. "I beg to differ."

Her nose edges closer to the ceiling. "It is honorable of you to defend your former employer. We will expect extreme loyalty here at WI-6. You may not discuss anything that happens here with anyone. I saw in the report you have no wife or girlfriend. That will make things easy for you."

The curt way she says it makes it obvious she means it as a dig. "Yes, I am unencumbered."

She pulls an iPad off her desk and hands it to me. "The forms are there for you to fill out." The squeak of plastic wheels on hardwood announce that the first part of my orientation is at an end. "You will follow me down to the media room where you will watch an orientation video. Place the device on the table when you leave." Then she turns on her high-heeled boots and marches back down the hallway.

Three doors further down I find the media room. When I open the door, I find the stark décor I expected in the lobby is in full display. She closes the door behind me, and I face a huge TV screen on the back wall and a bank of stackable plastic chairs like you see in museum viewing rooms. I'm getting the feeling that WI-6 only spends money where it counts. They wow you with the enormous skyscraper and the marble and black-mirrored building entrance. Yet in the inner spaces strictly for employees, spartan décor is the rule.

The screen flickers on and I push the iPad aside. The face of Mr. Bullock fills the screen. Once again, I'm struck by how Italian he looks. "Welcome to WI-6. You have been carefully selected to work as a detective in our division. It is an honor and an enormous responsibility. I hope you will treat the position with the reverence it deserves."

Boy, is he laying it on thick. Here I thought the Exemplary Wizard sounded puffed up when he spoke of the Twelfth Order.

Mr. Bullock steps back from the camera and snaps his fingers. A large screen slides down from the ceiling next to him. "There are only three rules you need to follow to be a good detective. Number one, trust your gut instincts. They will always do you a good service.

Number two, document everything you see and hear. During an investigation even the most trivial detail or offhand comment by a witness can help solve a case. I personally will give you a spell that will allow you to make copious notes in your head. Number three, trust dogs. Their senses are far better than ours."

The first two I can totally understand but number three. Trust dogs? What do they have to do with being a detective?

The rest of the orientation video consists of various rules of etiquette used at WI-6. Most of them we observed at the Twelfth Order as well, except one. The detective who solves their case must buy a round of drinks for the rest of the detectives. It seems a bit backwards at first, but when I think about it a bit more, it's undoubtedly the magnanimous thing to do.

My phone chirps letting me know I have a text. "Mr. Dunne your hour of torture is almost done. Finish up your forms and I will fetch you in ten minutes."

I breeze through the standard employment forms and quickly exit the media room and head back to the lobby.

Mrs. Hardcore darts out of her office. "I wish you luck, Mr. Dunne. I hope never to see you again." Mrs. Hardcore is living up to her name. She holds out her hand and I give her the iPad, hoping to never see her again either.

Scott greets me with a warm smile, then hands me a coffee cup. "Down that quick, you are going to need it. Mr. Bullock has asked for you to stop by his office."

The ride in the elevator is lightning quick as usual. I

step out but Scott remains inside. "I have something to do. You know the way."

I stride through the lobby and over to the executive office. Surprisingly, the door stands open. I straighten my tie and try to exude confidence. The first thing I notice is the awful plastic chair I endured on my first visit is noticeably absent. In its place is a black leather Parsons chair.

Mr. Bullock looks up from his computer screen. "Ah, Mr. Dunne. All signed up and ready to go?"

I sit down in the Parsons chair. "Yes, sir. I found the video quite interesting and helpful."

His eyebrows dart up. "Is that a good interesting or an interesting disguised as disapproval?"

I better redeem myself. "I found all the rules helpful. I especially look forward to learning the dictation spell. But..."

Mr. Bullock looks me in the eyes. "It's number three, isn't it? Do you have an aversion to dogs? Are you more of a cat man?"

The conversation is beyond odd, but I play along. "I never understood the whole notion that one must pick a side. Either you are team dog or team cat."

The corners of his mouth turn up slightly. "Interesting point. But you didn't answer the question."

"I like both equally, sir."

"Have you had a dog as a pet?"

This whole emphasis on dogs has me a bit worried. "Yes, I have. Although I do not possess one currently."

He sits up straighter in his chair. "Wonderful news."

"Sir?"

He snaps his fingers, and a large droopy eared sad faced black and tan bloodhound materializes next to him. "This is Holmes. He will be your right-hand dog while you are at WI-6."

I want to bolt out of my chair. The responsibility of a large dog is too much for me to handle. Tackling my own life is hard enough. Not to mention my small Craftsman bungalow in Santa Monica has barely enough room for me. "Are dogs a part of the WI-6 detective job description, sir?"

He beams, an obvious dog lover. "It is. And I would think you would be excited. I picked out a bloodhound for you due to your love of Sherlock Holmes novels."

My shoulders tense. The only way he could know that is by reading my mind. What else has he discovered about me through his exploration of my brain? I guess nothing too horrifying, or he wouldn't have hired me. "Yes, sir. I devoured Sherlock Homes novels when I was a kid. I'm also a fan of the series with Benedict Cumberbatch as Holmes."

He nods. "I think the show's interpretation of Mr. Holmes' various quirks were quite well done as well."

"Yes, I enjoyed it so much I watched all the seasons twice."

A large bit of drool escapes from Holmes's mouth. Mr. Bullock seems oblivious. "What do you think of your new hound?"

Watching Holmes use his large tongue to lick off any lingering drool, I don't know what to say. I spit out, "He's quite impressive." Mr. Bullock pets Holmes on his massive head. "Holmes, what do you think of your new owner?"

His large sad brown eyes look me up and down. In a perfect British boarding school accent he says, "Mr. Dunne seems a bit rough and tumble if you ask me."

The dog talks. Of course, he does. A wizard conjured him. I self-consciously run my fingers through my hair. "I'm usually a bit more pulled together."

Mr. Bullock snaps his fingers and Holmes flinches. "I wanted your dog to suit your personality and be a bit snarky himself, but I think I made him a bit too outspoken. I just tapped his snarkiness down a hair."

"Thank you, sir. It has been quite a while since I owned a dog, let alone one as large as Homes. May I ask how much food he will need every day? Also, my Craftsman bungalow is on a postage stamp sized lot. He won't have much room to move around."

Mr. Bullock beams. "You have no need to worry about the typical big dog chores such as several walks a day, having copious amounts of food on hand, and endless defecation clean up. Our dogs are burden-free."

I let out an audible sigh of relief having imagined the humongous bag of kibble I would need to buy weekly and the resulting damage the poops would do to the tiny patch of grass I call my backyard. "That is impressive magic, sir. Makes owning a dog even easier than a cat."

He laughs. "We at WI-6 try to think of anything we can do to make life easier for our detectives."

"It's much appreciated, sir."

He taps Holmes on his large shoulders. "Go to your owner. Serve him well."

Holmes nods and trots over to me. "At your service, Mr. Dunne."

I pat his large head wondering if I have a dog or a spy as my sidekick. "Thank you, Holmes. I look forward to working with you."

As if given a signal from his boss, Scott pops his head through the door. "Mr. Dunne, time for you to meet the detectives in *The Pit*."

I stand and Holmes heels next to me like we went through an eight-week dog training class together. Another benefit of a dog conjured by magic.

As I walk next to Scott with Holmes close to my side, I'm still curious about the whole dog as a detective companion thing. It reminds me so much of my witch friends and their familiars. "Why do the detectives at WI-6 need dogs as sidekicks?"

Scott chuckles as we enter the elevator. "It was Mr. Bullock's brilliant idea. He saw the strange bond Mr. Pierre had with his standard poodle, Fifi. His dog seemed to be able to read his mind. Fifi isn't a magical dog, so it got Mr. Bullock thinking. What if the detectives had more than just a wizard partner? K-9 dogs work so well for police, Mr. Bullock decided to make it part of the rules that all detectives at WI-6 should have their own dog. He spent many months conjuring different dogs and working out the kinks to create the perfect canine sidekick."

I look over at Holmes and flash on the science fiction movies where the robots find out they aren't real. Will Holmes be filled with resentment like the robots? Will our dogs' revolt against us? Man, I need a cup of coffee.

Scott hands me a coffee flavored protein bar. Is he another mind reader? "I want to give you a heads up before you meet the whole *Pit* crew. They are a very tough crowd. So don't take it personally if they snub you at first. It's been several years since a new detective has been brought in. Just give them some time."

Not exactly to the pep talk you want when you start a job, but I appreciate his honesty. "Got it. Tough crowd. Don't take the chilly reception personally."

Scott punches the elevator card key in the glowing slot. Then he presses the button for the thirtieth floor. Then he quickly steps back out of the elevator. "Good luck."

"It seems we are on our own." The elevator door closes, and I turn to Holmes. "Are you ready to meet our new colleagues?"

He looks up at me with his huge dark eyes. "Not particularly."

Seems Mr. Bullock's spell to tone down Holmes's snarkiness merely took the edge off. "I'm with you."

As the elevator doors open, I'm a bit startled when I see Mrs. Hardcore standing by the entrance of *The Pit*. She holds out a palm sized device. "Please sign here for the dog."

I scan the document, which makes me completely responsible for Holmes's welfare. If by chance things don't work out with WI-6, I am to return him in the same condition he was received. I sign the digital form and Mrs. Hardcore turns and runs for the elevator.

Holmes nudges me with his cold nose. "What was that about?"

I smile down at him. "You."

"Then I assume your ownership is official."

I bend down until we are eye to eye. "Let's get this straight. I don't own you. I am your caretaker. And if at any time you think I suck at it, you are free to leave."

There is a twinkle in his eyes. "Truly?"

"Yep. I'm totally serious."

Holmes nods. "Maybe you aren't as bad as I thought."

I decide to leave it at that and put my card key in the door slot for *The Pit*.

The door pops open to reveal the complete chaos of the normal workings of the detective division. Every desk is manned by my fellow detectives, including their obedient dog sidekicks. As *The Pit* is so dimly lit, I can't tell which breeds all the dogs are, reminding me I need to improve my vision. Before I can cast a visibility spell, I hear someone call out my name.

In a vaguely familiar French accent someone says, "Mr. Dunne, over here."

Mr. Pierre is standing next to a man who is built like a wrestler. Despite the low light the man's jet-black hair is gleams. "I'd like you to meet Detective Ross."

Ross pats the head of an enormous tan Mastiff then points to Holmes. "I see Mr. Bullock has conjured your dog. A bloodhound, classic detective choice."

I pat Holmes on the head. "Yes, he is. I'm quite pleased with him already."

Mr. Pierre nods. "Mr. Bullock takes the greatest of care to match the dogs to the detectives' personalities." He eyes a bit of drool escaping Holmes' mouth. "I take it you are a Sherlock Holmes fan."

"Yes, how did you know?"

He strokes his mustache like it's his beloved Fifi. "I have my ways." I gaze across the bustling room. "Seems there are quite a few cases at the moment."

Mr. Pierre nods. "Yes, there are. I will give you an orientation soon. But first I have someone I'd like you to meet." Mr. Pierre gestures to a person standing in the deepest recesses in the back of *The Pit*. "Mr. Dunne, I'd like you to meet your partner, Ms. Singh."

The woman lingers in the shadows for a moment before striding out into full view. I suck back a breath. No, it can't be. My new partner is the Indian woman I met last night.

5

SPY PARTNER

I don't know whether to be furious with my new partner or thrilled. She gives me a sly smile that makes me want to get to the bottom of her calling me up for a ride.

Mr. Pierre seems particularly pleased with his partner choice. "Ms. Singh is on temporary loan from the London office. She has some particularly unusual talents that will be useful to us."

Now I'm even more curious about her. It is hard to know how to play this as we have already met but my gut signals that my mysterious partner may not want anyone to know. I hold out my hand. "I'm Mr. Dunne. Nice to meet you Ms. Singh."

She smiles and shakes my hand. "I know you are new to being a detective, but you are in luck. I've been a detective at the London branch of WI-6 for four years."

Great. So, she is going to be my teacher. An attractive one to be sure. I'm disappointed Mr. Pierre felt I needed my hand held. Still, I can't complain about Ms. Singh as our time together in the car showed me, she is a kind person. Unless it was an act. Which I definitely need to find out sooner than later.

Mr. Pierre taps Mr. Ross's desk to get the rest of the detectives in *The Pit's* attention. "Can you please put down your work and stand by your desks so I can introduce you properly. The men and Ms. Burke do as they are instructed. Their dogs follow their owners leads. They stop milling around and move next to their prospective detective partners.

"Ms. Singh, this is Detective Ross and his dog Samson."

He must be the muscle of the division. I look at his sidekick, who's taller than his desk. Figures he'd have a Bull Mastiff as backup.

Ms. Singh nods. "Nice to meet you too."

Mr. Pierre moves over to the next desk. "This is Ms. Burke and her Labrador Miss Universe."

Singh's melodic laugh fills the air. "I love the name. She is quite the stunning chocolate lab."

Ms. Burke beams. "Thanks. I picked the name to drive the guys crazy. Glad we'll have some more estrogen in *The Pit*."

A low mutter escapes someone's lips. Mr. Pierre tugs at his mustache and glares at someone two desks down. We follow him over to the other side of the room. "This is Mr. Klein our senior detective and his Weimaraner, Manheim."

Mr. Klein's snow-white hair caps off a tall and lanky

body. Even though I can tell his suit is quite expensive, it hangs off his body like he bought it at a big box men's store. In a surprisingly deep voice he says, "Nice to meet you two. If you have any specific questions about how things are run around here, I'm your man."

Ms. Singh holds out her hand. "I will be sure to reach out if I need your help. I'm certain things are run a bit differently in the American division."

I follow suit and shake Mr. Klein's hand. I'm startled by his firm grip. "I will be sure I don't pester you too much."

He taps my shoulder. "I would appreciate that very much. The last rookie we had tried to become my conjoined twin."

I instantly like Mr. Klein. His sense of humor and humble demeanor makes me feel totally at ease.

Mr. Pierre moves to the far desk. "And last but certainly not least, our secret weapon. Mr. Smith and his pit bull Burt."

The first thing I notice about Mr. Smith is just like his name, he has a face that instantly looks familiar. One that you swear you've seen before. An everyman's face. His body type is equally average.

Ms. Singh holds out her hand. "Nice to meet you, secret weapon."

Darn that was going to be my line. "You are the division's everyman."

Mr. Smith nods. "Yes. I am a prosecutor's worst nightmare."

Mr. Pierre gives his shoulder a squeeze. "And a few attorney generals' as well."

I put on my best, *I'm so happy to meet you smile*. "It's wonderful meeting everyone. Thank you for allowing a newbie into *The Pit*."

Ross chimes in. "Don't wear out your welcome."

It gets a chuckle from Mr. Kline and Ms. Burke. I promise myself to do my best to not be a burden. I've trained a few wizards in Zoomer detail, and it can be exhausting when they ask too many questions.

Ms. Singh turns to Mr. Pierre. "Thank you so much for showing us around. We are ready to get right to work. I take it the empty desks are for us?"

"Yes, you assume correctly. I have taken the liberty to put all the current cases in a folder on your computers. After you both get oriented you can go home. We have an early morning meeting to go over the case I would like you to solve. Enjoy your last day of freedom. You will be quite busy after tomorrow."

The other detectives get back to work. *The Pit* is abuzz once again. As Ms. Singh moves toward her desk, I pull her aside. "We need to talk. I'll meet you in front of the bathrooms in two minutes."

She doesn't acknowledge my words. Instead, she pulls out her office chair and sits down. Terrific. She isn't going to tell me what last night was all about. She is going to learn I don't tolerate the silent treatment. I look down at my watch and as two minutes pass, I head out of the darkness of the pit and out the door. The bathrooms are just down a small hall. In a highly monitored workplace like *The Pit,* they must be a place of refuge.

I hover by the restroom for five minutes. When I am about to give up and return to my desk my partner arrives. I start to speak, but she holds up her hand. She points to her eyes and then to her ears. There must be a camera nearby. Of course, Mr. Bullock is spying on his own detectives. I smile and give her a thumbs up as I cast a privacy bubble spell. She looks around and can't see my magic. Good magic is always undetectable. "It's all right. I cast a spell that will protect us from probing eyes and ears."

Her beautifully arched brow stitches together. "Are you certain?"

"I can't be one hundred percent sure, but I do believe the spell is unique enough that even the WI-6 cannot penetrate it. The Twelfth Order wizards are just as powerful in their own way."

She nods and smiles. "What is so important you would risk using unauthorized magic?"

"Why did you pretend not to know me when I picked you up on Melrose. Were you doing your own sleuthing?"

Her eyes twinkle. "First off, we don't know each other. The second is, can you blame me for being curious about my new partner? I wanted to make sure you weren't, as you Americans say, a jerk."

I laugh. "A woman can't be too careful."

She flicks her long hair over her shoulders. "Precisely. "

"We should probably head back but I'm curious why you weren't given a dog."

A shy smile crosses her lips. "You are a detective

now. I'm sure you can find out through your newfound skills."

I break the bubble and she strolls into the bathroom. So, she is going to play hard to get. I'm game.

§.

INSTEAD OF THE WELL-DESERVED BREAK MR. PIERRE spoke of I have been summoned to the Twelfth Order headquarters. I look in the rearview mirror at Holmes drooling all over my leather back seat and wonder just what I have gotten myself into. Driving into the underground tunnel Order parking for the last time, it feels anti-climactic. I yearned for a change, but I will miss my colleagues at the Order. Especial Mr. Kumar who has been a wonderful boss.

Holmes barks when I stop the car. "This is where you used to work? In the underground?"

His British sensibilities are starting to grow on me. "Yes. The Twelfth Order is in charge of making sure all the major cities of the world don't self-destruct."

"Interesting. I was told you did reconnaissance."

"Yes, under the guise of being a Zoomer driver."

He sits up and looks at me in the rearview mirror. "And you didn't feel it was beneath you?"

I open the door for him. "I did at first, but I enjoy people. Zoomer driving gave me a break from when I was working."

He follows next to me as we enter the elevator. "You are a better person than I."

I want to laugh, but stuff it down. The robots and

their rebellion are still on my mind. If he thinks of himself like a person, who am I to argue?

When the elevator door opens to reveal the blinking lights and chaos of the Order headquarters, I understand why Holmes' head is swiveling in all directions. His nose twitches at the overpowering fragrance of roses. "Interesting. The Twelfth Orders' magic smells like roses. I would have thought all wizards' magic smelled alike."

I patted him on the head. "Yes, I thought the same thing until I smelled peonies at the WI-6 headquarters."

A smiling Mr. Kumar greets us. "Good to see you, Derrick." He looks down at my Bloodhound sidekick. "And who do we have here?"

"This is Holmes. The detectives at WI-6 all have dogs as sidekicks. Say hello to Mr. Kumar."

Holmes glances up at my boss. "It is a pleasure to meet you."

Mr. Kumar chuckles. "A talking dog with a British accent no less. I would expect nothing less from WI-6."

Holmes puffs out his chest. "It is an honor to work for such powerful wizards."

"I'm sure it is." Mr. Kumar leads us down the main tunnel to one of the meeting rooms. "We just need to debrief you."

He crouches down to Holmes's height. "If you don't mind, I need borrow Derrick for a while. Is there someplace you would like to go while you wait?"

Holmes looks perplexed. "You want me to go some-where else?"

Mr. Kumar smiles. "I don't want you to get bored. It could be at least an hour wait."

I better step in. "Holmes, wizards of the Twelfth Order are time masters. Mr. Kumar can transport you to any place you like while you wait for me."

Holmes nods. "If that is the case, I have so wanted to visit Doheny Beach. I read the beach hosts the most astounding number of sea gulls."

Mr. Kumar snaps his fingers. "Brilliant choice. Doheny Beach is lovely this time of day. Enjoy yourself."

And just like that Holmes vanishes in a thin veil of lavender mist. "That was very considerate of you, sir. I'm sure he would have been bored just sitting around waiting for me."

"It is no trouble. I hope he enjoys chasing the seagulls."

We both chuckle as I follow Mr. Kumar to one of the meeting rooms. As he opens the door, I realize this may be the last time I see him. "Sir, I just wanted to say before we start the debriefing that I am going to miss you. It has been a pleasure to work under you."

He sits down in the chair next to me. "The feeling is mutual. It has been my great pleasure to watch you grow into a man."

I laugh. "Was I really that much of a handful when I first came to the Order?"

"A bit, but you tamed down nicely."

A pang of loss hit me. I really was going to miss him. "Gee, thanks."

He snapped his finger and the viewing screen in front of us lights up. Thankfully the face of the Exemplary Wizard didn't appear. Instead, a long list of the various disasters in Los Angeles that I'd played a part in stopping. Had it really been over fifty incidents?

Mr. Kumar's gaze shifts from me to the screen. "You've had quite a lot of accomplishments during your time at the Order. Which one sticks in your memory?"

"There have been so many it is a bit of a blur but two come to mind. The day we vanquished Murdock and his vampires, and the day we got rid of the dark elves." A pain hits my heart at the memory of Tara and how she escaped death from the dark elves only to be killed by a rival witch.

Mr. Kumar's brow furrows. "You still miss her, don't you?"

"Yes, sir, I do. I know it has been almost a year but still..."

He nods. "Yes, the pain of losing your first love runs deep."

He says it with such depth of feeling I know he has lost someone special too. By the lingering pain in his voice, it was not all that long ago. I wonder if it was someone back in India. Mr. Kumar is a private person so I will never know. "Thank you for caring, sir. I know I was not easy to deal with right after her death."

He pats my hand. "You never let the Order down, only yourself."

Mr. Kumar has been far more than my boss; he was

the father I wish I had. "Truth."

He snaps his fingers and the screen changes to purple, the color of the Twelfth Order's magic.

"I am happy that you are becoming a detective for WI-6. I think you are very well suited for it."

I smile and say, "But..."

He chuckles. "As the screen denotes, the Twelfth Order's magic is ours alone. Once you leave the umbrella of the Order your magic will be greatly diminished. At WI-6 you will learn new magic, but they will only reveal things slowly, as we did here."

I nod. "Yes, I understand." Holding my hand over my heart I say, "I promise not to reveal anything I've learned here."

"I know you mean what you say, Derrick, I truly do. But we need to guarantee it. Information could be taken without your knowledge. The wizards of WI-6 are known to be quite persistent in getting what they want."

Mr. Kumar places his strong hands on either side of my head, and I wonder what am I getting myself into? My neck stiffens at the thought this might be a huge mistake. "Promise it won't affect my brain's function."

His hands feel like warm washcloths on either side of my head. "I promise. This will actually protect your brain from ever being compromised."

I nod and feel a warm sensation radiating across my scalp like it had been wrapped in a heating pad. My mind goes blank for just a second, but I don't panic. I trust Mr. Kumar implicitly. I run the alphabet through my mind along with a few spells and know it is backfiring on all cylinders. I supposed I should be offended that I am not trusted to keep the Twelfth Order's secrets. Yet, I feel relieved.

Mr. Kumar removes his hands and smiles. "I'm glad you think of it that way. I only did it for your protection."

Of course, he read my mind. "Is there anything else you need from me? I place the Beemer car keys on the conference table along with my headquarters access key card.

Mr. Kumar shakes his head and pushes the BMW keys back toward me. "The car is a gift for your years of service to the Order. "

Sensing our time together is at an end, I stand up. Clutching the BMW keys, I'm eternally grateful for his gracious gift. "Thank you so much, sir."

He places his hand on my shoulder. "We are keeping your Zoomer account open as well. I know some of your friends only have that way to find you."

Funny, I never thought about the special Zoomer number the Order created just for me. I would hate to lose touch with some of my paranormal friends, but he is right. "You've been way too kind, sir." In fact, his kindness makes me feel more than a little bit guilty for leaving. We exit the meeting room and Mr. Kumar snaps his fingers. Holmes materializes dripping wet with a piece of seaweed stuck to one of his back paws. I pat him on the head. "It looks like you had a fun time."

He grins up at Mr. Kumar. "Doheny Beach is a truly marvelous place. The articles I read were correct. The seagulls were plentiful."

Mr. Kumar chuckles. "Did you catch one?"

Holmes snorts. "No, but I truly enjoyed trying."

I TURN THE KEY ON THE WOOD PANELED DOOR OF MY little bungalow. The faint hint of salt in the air reminds me how lucky I am to live mere blocks from the ocean. Holmes trots into the combination living room, dining room, with enthusiasm. I'm suddenly a bit embarrassed by just how small the bungalow is. "It's not very big, but it's home."

Holmes looks around my nine hundred and fifty square foot bungalow. "I think it is quite charming. The Craftsman detail is evident in the coffered ceiling in the dining room and the built-in buffet. Also, the classic Batchelder tiles on the fireplace." He moves closer to the tiles. "I see one depicts a yucca plant blooming, the other a cactus, and the center tile depicts the San Gabriel Mountains at sunset."

Wow. I can't believe it. Holmes picked out all the details that made me fall in love with the little Craftsman bungalow. Not to mention its location. "You seem to enjoy Craftsman architectural details as much as I do. They were very popular a few years back but not so much now. But I still love my place."

"As you should. It is quite attractive."

Somehow his stuffy British boarding school accent fits right in with the style of the home. The Craftsman movement started in England after all. I walk over to the kitchen desperate for a drink of water and a snack.

I reach into the cupboard and instantly feel guilty. "Holmes, do you eat and drink?" As soon as it comes out of my mouth, I feel like an idiot. Mr. Bullock already told me the dogs he created were magical and very low maintenance.

Holmes gives me a disapproving stare as I open a bag of cashews and pour some in a glass bowl. "We can eat a treat or two if that is what you are asking."

I grab a handful of nuts. "Great, how about these?"

He shakes his massive head. "No thank you. But I do like peanut butter if it is organic." He gets a contemplative look on his face. "I prefer a good roasted femur bone from a grass-fed cow."

It seems Homes is a bit of a health nut. "Got it." I snap my fingers and the requested grass-fed cow bone appears at his feet.

He looks down and barks approvingly. "I must say there are distinct advantages to having a wizard as an owner."

I ignore the fact that he called me his owner once again even after my lecture. "And do you have any sleeping preferences?"

He eyes my Craftsman leather sofa and chairs that I admit are more for looks than comfort. "Is it possible I could procure a comfortable sofa of my own?"

I laugh. "Are you doubting my conjuring abilities?"

He looks down at the humongous dog bone. "Not at all."

"Good." I snap my fingers and a large dog-sized plush blue velvet sofa appears near the front door. It is the only free space I have in the house where it can fit. "There you go."

He picks up his bone and trots over to the sofa. "Thank you. Do you mind if I take a nap? It has been quite an exhausting day."

Not having had a dog in a while, I can't remember how much they sleep, but I know it's way more than humans or wizards. "Sure, take it easy. I'll try not to make too much noise."

He snorts. "You can be as loud as you wish. We large dogs tend to sleep like the dead."

Chuckling I say, "I bet you do. It's a good thing because this is a small house."

He jumps up on his doggie sofa, takes a couple of chews on his bone, and is snoring in minutes. There is something endearing about the way his large ears drape over the edge of the sofa cushion like a shawl. Looking at him with drool dripping out of the corner of his mouth, I realize just how big of a hole in my heart Tara left.

Maybe fate has decided to be kind to me with this new job. With Holmes in residence, it will be hard to feel lonely. Yet, something about having him here makes me feel uneasy. Why did Mr. Kumar feel the need to send him off to Doheny Beach? Holmes could have just as easily waited for me outside the meeting room. He probably would have fallen asleep like he is now. Then the nagging reason hits me like a baseball bat to my head. Mr. Kumar wanted Holmes gone for a good reason. He is the eyes and ears of his creator— Mr. Bullock.

6

THE KILLER LIST

On the drive to wI-6 headquarters the bright sunshine makes me squint. Having not slept much last night I'm beyond light sensitive. Holmes, on the other hand, lays on the back seat with his legs in the air snoring. My revelation about him last night makes me wonder how we will navigate our relationship. Maybe I can come up with a spell to shield his mind from Mr. Bullock as Mr. Kumar did for me. That should be at the top of my priority list. I dial Mr. Kumar's number. Surprisingly, he answers on the third ring. "Sir, this is Derrick, I know I am not supposed to use Order magic any longer, but this is really important."

"You figured out the problem with Holmes."

"I did, sir. And I feel quite foolish for bringing him to headquarters. I keep thinking of him as if he's a regular dog."

Kumar sighs. "He is anything but."

"Exactly, which is why I called."

Mr. Kumar clears his throat and hesitates to answer. I wonder if my phone is bugged. "You don't have to worry about your dog causing problems or being bugged. We took care of that the second we knew you were getting the job."

Maybe his hesitation is admitting that despite the seemingly friendly relationship between the Exemplary Wizard and Mr. Bullock, the distrust is still there.

I shouldn't be surprised, yet I am. Wizards tend to distrust others of their kind who are not in their circle.

"Thank you for watching my back."

Mr. Kumar chuckles. "You can thank me for one more thing."

"I'd be happy too if I knew what it is."

"Holmes is under the influence of a sleeping spell."

I stand in the dark depths of *The Pit* watching my new colleagues start their day. By the way they eye me as I walk by, they probably don't trust me as far as they can throw me. I need to make an extra effort to help them feel at ease around me. I really do want to make *The Pit* my new home and put my Zoomer reconnaissance days behind me.

The fragrance of Shalimar fills the air as Ms. Singh strolls through the door wearing a perfectly tailored black pants suit, a crisp white shirt, and a killer pair of pointed toe black leather boots. If she's trying to fit in with the boys, she's failing. Her long flowing mane of shiny black hair hangs down almost to her waist. Somehow it seems even longer than the first time I saw her. A painful tinge of recognition hits me at how similar her hair is to Tara's. She strides up to me with the confidence of someone who had a good night's sleep and knows they are good at their job. Both of which I'm lacking.

"Mr. Dunne, those dark circles under your eyes tell me you had a hard night."

Holmes sits by my side wide awake thanks to his sleeping spell wearing off. He can't resist chiming in. "I think he is a bit apprehensive about starting the new job."

I tap Holmes on his massive head. "As you can see, my sidekick has a lot of confidence in my abilities."

Ms. Singh cracks a smile making me take notice of the flattering lip color she has on—a nice shade of mauve. "Have no fear. I'm here to guide your way."

Some guys would make some crack about guiding her to their place, but as attractive as she is, I know better than to mix business with pleasure. "Good. Because I know I'm going to need it."

She moves toward her desk with the silence of a leopard stalking its prey. I flow along next to her with Holmes bringing up the rear.

Ms. Singh turns to me and says, "I saw your evaluation and your job skills report. It was impressive. You'll get in the swing of being a detective in no time."

The fact that she knows so much about me, and I know next to nothing about her is a bit unsettling. It makes me more determined than ever to learn more about her.

Ms. Singh looks over at Holmes. "Your sidekick needs to get on board."

Holmes's nose twitches. "What is that delectable fragrance you are wearing?" I'm impressed a dog has such a command of the art of conversational evasion.

"It's called Shalimar." She smiles at Holmes like a cat that ate a pet bird. "Good on you for trying to evade my statement about your lack of support for your owner. Too bad it didn't work."

Holmes puffs out his chest. "I will have you know I am dedicated to aiding in Mr. Dunne's job improvement."

I hold up my hands between them like a bouncer. "Guys, it's only my first official day. Cut me some slack."

Mr. Pierre strides over to where we are standing. "I would like to see you both in the conference room in five minutes."

Ms. Singh gives my shoulder an encouraging squeeze. "Are you ready for your first assignment?"

I look around the vast dark space of *The Pit*. "If someone will show me where the conference room is."

A series of low chuckles turn into outright laughter at my expense.

Ms. Burke stifles a laugh as she approaches me. "I'll be happy to show you where it is."

Not the way I wanted to start my first day as the butt of a joke, but at least I'm memorable.

Ms. Singh moves next to Ms. Burke. "It is nice of you to show us the way. I must admit I have no idea where the conference room is located either."

I crack a satisfied smile. Ms. Singh really does have my back. We move to the deepest part of *The Pit* where Mr. Pierre has his desk. He seems to be MIA. Another unexplained disappearance.

Ms. Burke snaps her fingers, and a door materializes. "The guys wanted to test you right off the bat."

Ms. Singh turns and glares back into the darkness as the muffled sound of our fellow detectives chuckling can still be heard. "I'd hoped we wouldn't get pranked. But that was expecting too much from you Americans."

I'm liking my partner more and more. "Touché Ms. Singh."

A sigh escapes Ms. Burke's bright red lips. "I'm sorry. It wasn't my idea. The guys just couldn't help themselves."

"Apparently," Ms. Singh says in a disdainful voice.

"Go have a seat." Ms. Burke motions to the brightly lit conference room. "Mr. Pierre will be with you shortly."

I take the leather office chair nearest the door. "Thanks for backing me up."

She gracefully slides into the chair next to me. "I will always defend my partner."

"Likewise." I lean back in my chair glad to be out of the line of fire if just for a few minutes. "Have you noticed the top wizards of WI-6 have a habit of disappearing?"

She gracefully crosses her long legs at the ankle. There is something innately sexy about it. "Yes, I have. But it is no different at the UK division. I think they are all full of bluster."

There is something about the way British people speak that makes me smile. "They certainly are."

As if on cue, Mr. Pierre materializes behind the chair at the head of the long glass conference table. "Good morning team DS." His gaze shifts to me. "Someone looks a bit sleep deprived."

Team DS has a nice ring to it I think as I run my fingers through my hair. As if the sheer act could hide the dark circles under my eyes. "It's true I didn't have the best night's sleep. To be honest, I was a bundle of nerves about my first day."

He strokes his mustache. "Honesty is a keynote of how WI-6 operates."

Ms. Singh nods. "The saying honesty is the best policy exists for a reason."

Mr. Pierre eyes Holmes who is lying by my feet. "How are you adjusting to having a dog, Mr. Dunne?"

"Holmes is pretty hassle free as you promised. Although he still has his snarky edge."

His eyes narrow in on Holmes who lets out a loud snoring sound pretending to be asleep. "Do you wish me to alter his personality?"

I shake my head. "No. I think he is going to make life more interesting this way. I don't want a yes dog as a sidekick."

Ms. Singh chuckles as Holmes stops feigning sleep and chimes in. "I am glad you feel that way. Because I like me just the way I am."

The room fills with laughter even from Mr. Pierre. He smiles down at Holmes. "Did you get that from a TV commercial?"

Holmes looks indignant. "No. The line is all mine."

I would get a dog that is full of himself.

Mr. Pierre snaps his fingers, and a large viewing screen drops down from the ceiling. The face of a thin man with freckles on his nose high, cheek bones, and bright blue eyes fills the screen. "This is Peter Hamlyn. He was a wizard from Serenity."

Ms. Singh lines forward in the chair taking in the man's face. "Was?"

Mr. Pierre nods. "He died unexpectedly ten days ago."

Now I know the reason why I'm at WI-6. "And you think his death is suspicious."

"Yes. Mr. Hamlyn was a health nut and only thirty-eight years old. An infant in wizard years." He eyes Ms. Singh leaning forward getting ready to say something. "And before you ask, he was not working on anything when he died."

"Was he on vacation?" Ms. Singh asks.

"No. On his off hours he was a chef at a vegan restaurant he founded. When he died, he was talking to the sous chef and seemed fine. Then he gasped for breath and suddenly became unconscious. They could not resuscitate him even with the use of magic."

Ms. Singh lets out an audible sigh. "Tragic for someone so young."

It sounds funny from a woman that looks to be in her late twenties. "I take that Mr. Hamlyn's death is to be our first investigation."

Mr. Pierre nods. "Yes. Something tells me this is not a standard natural death case, so I wanted fresh eyes on it."

Ms. Singh leans back in her chair. "So that explains why I had to fly out of London so quickly."

"Yes, the trail is already getting cold. I want you to meet with our wizard examiner. If after your meeting with him, you agree that there is possible foul play I want you to put together a killer list."

My mouth goes dry. "A list of suspects you mean?"

Mr. Pierre's mustache twitches. "We at WI-6 like to call it as we see it. It is a list of possible killers."

Ms. Singh smiles. "I like it."

Mr. Pierre stands up and hands Ms. Singh a key card. "This has everything you need. The examiner's location and it is also the access key to the resting place."

My brow furrows. "Sir?"

He smiles. "Resting place sounds so much nicer than the morgue."

I STAND WITH MY NEW PARTNER IN THE MIDDLE OF the final resting place. It looks exactly like the medical examining rooms you see on TV, except the autopsy is done through magic.

The wizard examiner stands over Peter Hamlyn's body. "I have done a thorough examination and I can find nothing to explain his death except one thing. His vitamin A count was through the roof."

Ms. Singh eyes his obviously yellow skin. "Did he have a drinking problem? This kind of coloration usually denotes an alcoholic with cirrhosis of the liver."

It appears my partner has no problem showing off she has far more experience than I do. I need to learn to not feel slighted.

The wizard examiner nods. "Yes, that would have been my conclusion too. Yet, my tests revealed Mr. Hamlyn had no alcohol in his system. He also had no other signs of disease in his body."

Thinking back to the brief bio on Mr. Hamlyn that Mr. Pierre gave us, it sparks an idea. "It is my understanding that Mr. Hamlyn was quite the health nut. He had a vegan restaurant and lectured other wizards on healthy eating. Don't you think someone who understood supplements and nutrition would know better than to overdo vitamin A?"

The examiner nods. "Yes, one would think so. That was why I was surprised at the unbelievably high amount of vitamin A in his system. I understand he was an avid juicer. A large carrot has 510 micrograms of A. He would have to eat one hundred and fifty carrots to hit that number. There is a slight possibility he might have been killed by consuming carrots."

I laugh. "You have to be joking."

Ms. Singh ignores my outburst and looks down on Peter Hamlyn with concern on her face. "Then we are to assume this death was actually a murder?"

"I cannot say for certain. He could have developed an allergy to vitamin A. But it does seem quite an odd death."

Odd is right up my alley. "Thank you for reviewing Mr. Hamlyn's case."

The examiner covers the body with a space type blanket. "I am always at the service of WI-6."

We leave the morgue and Ms. Singh pulls me aside. "I'm certain this is a murder. We had a few unusual wizard deaths in London, but no one took them seriously. I'm not going to let that happen again. For all I know this could be the same murderer who just moved across the pond to do his dirty work."

I open the door to my Beemer for her. "My gut tells me you are right. "

Ms. Singh smiles as she slides into the passenger seat. "Now all we have to do is prove it."

Placing my hands on the steering wheel, I give her a quick smile. "Sounds like a piece of cake."

"Do you mean as easy as pie?"

I laugh. "I guess we will have to learn each other's slang."

"True, enough." She reaches into her purse and pulls out her phone. "I'll start making notes."

"That is quite the impressive handbag. I believe it's a Burberry Bayswater."

Her eyes grow wide. "How do you know that?"

I give her a satisfied grin, knowing I've surprised

her. "I have a friend who owns every British designer bag you can think of." I should thank Krissy the next time I see her for my knowledge of British designer handbags. Something I never thought I would need until now.

"Mr. Dunne, you are full of surprises."

"Please call me Derrick when we are out in the field."

She gives me a side eye. "Isn't that against WI-6 protocol?"

I start the engine. "I'm not the type to stand by protocol. Are you?"

"Usually. But I'm in America now so I might as well follow the natives." She holds her hand out to me. "My name is Fiona."

A classic British name. I shake her hand. "Where to Fiona?"

She leans back in her seat. "The vegan restaurant."

"Brilliant idea." I punch the address into my GPS, and we head over to the Westside of town. After ten minutes of silence with Fiona texting away while I drive down the freeway, she finally stops and looks up.

"Mr. Dunne...excuse me Derrick, I'd like to go over how we plan to interview witnesses. Would you like me to take the women or the men?"

I think about it for a moment. "Why not interview them together at first? If someone seems to respond better to you, then I will step away and let you take the lead."

"That is very generous of you."

From some people that would be a sarcastic line,

but from Fiona I know it's sincere. "It's not being generous, it's just common sense. You are the more experienced detective. Heck, I have no experience at all."

She chuckles. "You keep forgetting I saw your report. The work you did for the Twelfth Order was quite impressive. If you are in the front lines of a reconnaissance mission, you are a natural detective."

I have no idea why she is being so kind, but I'll take it. "Thanks. I'll do my best not to embarrass you."

She goes back to texting someone while I dodge major LA traffic to get to the restaurant. Ironically, the place is not far from Wick and Scone. It's in a similarly trendy Westside location. I pull up to the curb and get my debit card ready to take the usual parking meter hit. Fiona doesn't seem to notice that the car has stopped.

She looks up from her phone. "We're here so quickly?"

I smile. "I'm a former Zoomer driver, if you recall."

She smiles and stashes her phone in her Burberry bag. "Of course, you know all the shortcuts in Los Angeles."

I put my hand on my trusty Beemer steering wheel. "I like to think so."

Fiona opens the passenger side door and I instinctively fly out the driver's side door and race over to help her out of the car.

She beams at me. "Thank you for being a proper gentleman."

Hearing her boarding school British accent makes me want to bow. Instead, I lock up the car, pay the parking meter, and hold the restaurant door open for her.

She laughs. "All right, now you are just showing off."

We walk inside the stark white decorated restaurant to find not one customer. Only a hostess at the stand dressed in a white shift dress to match the décor. "Are you the detectives?"

How could she know that? I look at Fiona, puzzled, but she ignores me. "Yes, we are. Is everyone I requested here?"

Here is my answer to who she was texting. The hostess looks down at a list on the hostess stand. "Everyone but Brandon, the dishwasher. He already has a new gig."

Fiona motions to the hostess. "Let's take you first, Miss Lake. Where would you like to talk?"

Looks like Fiona is taking the lead. Fine with me. It gives me a chance to use the dictation spell. Besides, she's the one with experience. I have no trouble sitting back and learning from her.

The hostess gazes out at the empty restaurant. Then she points to a table toward the juice bar along the far wall. "Here is fine."

Sitting down at the table Fiona looks down at a note on her phone. "Miss Lake, I understand you have worked at the Health Nut for two years."

I lean back in my chair in a bit of shock that a wizard named his vegan restaurant Health Nut. No wonder there was a giant nut shaped sign hanging over the door.

Ms. Lake fidgets in her white wire chair. "Yes, for

almost two years. Peter was a great boss. Super funny and he was always doing magic tricks with vegetables. The customers loved it."

It's ironic how we wizards pose as magicians to hide our magic.

Fiona makes a note on her phone. "How many regular customers did you have?"

The hostess's brow furrows, and I notice she has a tiny diamond stud through her right brow. "It was a popular restaurant. I'd say we had at least fifty."

I decide to cut in. "Why do you keep talking about the restaurant in the past tense? Mr. Hamlyn didn't have any partners?"

She sighs. "No, he didn't. It sucks cause the crew here is tight, like a family, you know. Now we all must find new jobs. The estate lawyer told us to clean out everything by tomorrow."

Fiona chimes in. "Did the lawyer say anything about someone wanting to purchase the restaurant space?"

She frowns. "Yes, that is why we have to be out by tomorrow night. Someone bought the space already."

I'm not surprised at all. Storefronts fly off the market in trendy LA neighborhoods like this one.

Fiona stands up. "Thank you, Miss. Lake. Can you send out the sous chef Mr. Hardy next?"

Miss. Lake pushes back her chair and speeds walks over to the swinging door off to the left side of the juice bar.

Fiona kicks my leg under the table. "Ouch," I say and rub my shin. "What did you do that for?"

"I know you are new to being a detective, but never

interrupt my questioning without giving me a signal first."

"A jab in the shin with your killer pointed boots is a bit extreme."

She smiles. "It made an impression on you, didn't it?" A bald guy with a large pot belly that is stretching his apron strings to the point of ripping off, moves toward us. If you had a wanted poster for a possible killer, this guy would be on it. The sous chef looks like he's done time.

He casually pulls out his chair like we are old friends. Something tells me being interviewed by cops isn't new to him. "Okay. Let's get this over with. I have to finish breaking down the kitchen equipment tonight."

Fiona doesn't miss a beat. "I thought the restaurant was sold. Usually, the new owner wants all the equipment."

He rubs the top of his head. "Yeah, that would make sense but the guy who bought it is some hot shot up and coming chef who wants everything to be brand new."

The new owner has an interesting quirk. I nudge Fiona's foot signaling I want a stab at the guy. "We won't keep you long. I just have a few questions. As the sou chef you worked closely with Peter in the kitchen. Did he ever mention anything about having someone who was mad at him?"

He glared at me. "You trying to tell me he was murdered? They said it was a natural death. Something about heart issues in the family."

Talk about a fabricated story. "Who told you that?"

"That lawyer guy who is running the show. I gave him some lip and he said he'd tell my parole officer."

Fiona and I look at each other and smile. We just found ourselves the number one candidate for our killer list.

7

THE MYSTERY DEEPENS

Back in the familiar office of the top man at WI-6, Fiona gives me a wink. "We must have done something right if Mr. Bullock asked to see us."

She doesn't question why or what he might have learned from spying on us. I had to admire her concentration on the task at hand. Finding the person who murdered Peter Hamlyn is our priority. Which made me hope that our meeting with Mr. Bullock would be quick so we could question the lawyer. Although he hadn't responded to Fiona's phone call for an appointment yet.

Sitting in the office without Holmes feels strange. It was the place we first met. But Mr. Bullock made a specific request for me not to bring Holmes. This time Mr. Bullock doesn't even try to hide his magic. One minute we were sitting in our chairs facing a walnut desk with no one behind it. The next Mr. Bullock is sitting behind the desk staring back at us. I had to smile at the fact that, although he looked impeccably dressed as always, his mustache was a bit ruffled from his journey through time and space.

"I called you here because I heard through the grapevine that you had some success with your interviews at the Health Nut."

I see Fiona's shoulders tighten at his words. Could she have finally figured out Mr. Bullock is using magic to track our progress? At first, I felt violated, but then I realized he must use surveillance to spy on all his new detectives. He did say he ran a tight ship.

Fiona sits silent, still absorbing the news of being spied on, so I jump in. "Yes, sir. We did make some good progress with the Peter Hamlyn investigation. It seems Mr. Hamlyn's estate lawyer has very specific orders from a will. Yet, I find it hard to believe that someone as young and health focused as Mr. Hamlyn, would ever think to draw one up. I know I sure haven't."

Mr. Bullock strokes his mustache. "It does seem quite odd. But then again, he did have a business to protect."

Mr. Bullock does have a point.

"I assume that is your next destination?"

Fiona finally comes out of her stupor. "Yes, I have put in a request for an appointment, but we haven't heard from him. If he continues to ignore my call, we will show up at his office unannounced. He's hiding something."

Mr. Bullock nods. "Good. Never accept no for an answer. Which leads me to why I asked you both here.

I'm certain by now you have realized I cast a surveillance spell on both of you."

Might as well show I'm not as much of a newbie as he might think. "I have, sir. I'm sure you have your reasons. As you can tell, I have nothing to hide."

Fiona purses her lips. "I can understand you placing one on Mr. Dunne. He is a rookie after all. But me?"

Her words sting a bit. I hope it is just for show and she really doesn't think of me as some loser rookie.

Mr. Bullock sits up a bit straighter in his chair. "I actually had no qualms about leaving you to your own devices. The request for the spell came from your London office."

Fiona slams her fist on the arm of her chair. "The audacity. May I be excused?"

Mr. Bullock nods. "Of course. I'm more than happy to lift the spell if you can get permission."

She storms out of the office, and I fight back a smile. Fiona is beyond sexy when she gets mad.

Mr. Bullock twists the tip of his mustache. "You have quite the fiery partner Mr. Dunne. Not that I blame her for being upset. She has far too much experience to be babysat."

"I agree. Having worked with her all day, she is the epitome of professional."

Mr. Bullock lets out a chuckle. "Except for the kick in the shin."

"Right," I say, still feeling the lump on my leg throb a bit. "Was there anything else, sir?"

"Yes, this case seems to be growing legs. I want you

to be suspicious of everyone at this point. Something is very amiss. My gut is on fire."

"I agree, sir. Nothing seems to be adding up."

Fiona strides back into the room with flushed cheeks. I would hate to have been the person she just got off the phone with. She glances down at her watch. "Sir, we need to go. The lawyer refused to respond to my call. We will head there next."

Mr. Bullock stands up from his desk. I'm a bit surprised he didn't vanish as usual. "If anything doesn't feel right, don't hesitate to call in for backup."

Fiona picks up her purse and turns toward the door. "There will be no need for us to call. Your surveillance spell will tell you if we are in over our heads."

❧

FIONA SITS NEXT TO ME IN THE BEEMER muttering to herself in Hindi. "I'm a great listener if you want to talk."

She stops muttering to herself. "We are partners, but can I truly trust you?"

I'd be offended if I didn't know she was so upset. She's just transferring her trust issues onto me. Hoping to cheer her up, I place my hand over my heart. "I swear on my life as a wizard, I will never repeat anything you tell me."

She lets out a deep yoga breath. "The reason why the London branch wanted Mr. Bullock to cast a surveillance spell is they didn't trust that I would be allowed to give them information about our case."

I turn down Pico Boulevard feeling like I'm going to regret what I'm about to say. "Isn't our work supposed to stay here in America?"

"Yes, but now that we know there are unusual wizard deaths on both sides of the pond, it might be beneficial to coordinate our information. The surveillance spell is Mr. Bullock's way of cooperating."

Now I know why she is so hurt. "So, you are ticked off that your boss felt the need to go over your head."

"Precisely. I could have negotiated the information sharing myself. I'm totally capable."

"Look, I know it must sting, but you have to let it go. We have an important investigation to complete."

She nods and pulls out her phone. "You probably just saved my job." Her fingers fly across her phone. "If I had sent this text to my superior, I would be flying back to Delhi, not London."

"I've always got your back, remember?"

She nods. "I know."

A call buzzes through my screen. "Mr. Dunne. Don't bother to go to the lawyer's office. He took off."

Ms. Burke must be on our side. "Right. Let us know when you locate him. We need to talk to him ASAP."

"Will do. For now, why don't you head back over to the restaurant? One of the people on your list showed up there."

There is something decidedly unsettling about the layers of surveillance at WI-6. Yet, I must admit it should make things much easier for Team DS.

Fiona chimes in. "So, the dishwasher finally showed up?"

Ms. Burke's sultry voice fills the car. "Yes. If I were you, I'd get over there pronto before he disappears again?"

Fiona sighs. "I knew there were going to be disadvantages to being partnered with a rookie, but this amount of micromanaging is an insult to my years of experience as a detective."

She sure knows how to make a guy feel like a ten-year-old that needs supervision on the playground. "I'm sorry you've been saddled with me. You can request a transfer back to London."

She reaches over and touches my hand that is resting on the center console. Despite that fact she has just belittled me big time, I can feel the pull of attraction from her touch.

"I'm sorry. You must think I'm one royal class, how do you say it in America, bitch. I shouldn't take my bruised ego out on you."

I pull up to the restaurant noticing it's missing something important. Hoping for a smile from Fiona I say, "Look, the restaurant has lost its nut."

One of the corners of her mouth turns up. "What an astute observation. Should we change our assignment to the case of the missing nut?"

Happy to see her pretty smile return, I hold the door open for her. Amazing what a few hours can do. All the furniture is missing, and two construction guys are busy ripping out the juice bar. The hostess has long left the premises. We walk around the scattered debris of the former juice bar and head back to the kitchen. We push open the door to find most of the equipment is gone along with the ex-con sous chef. A man with blonde slightly spiked hair is busy taking apart the dishwashing equipment. I move next to him. "Hi, do you have a minute? We are investigating Mr. Hamlyn's death."

The man looks up, sweat pouring down his chiseled face. He looks more like a male model or an actor than a dishwasher. "If you haven't figured it out, he was murdered. I found the body. There was no way his death was from natural causes."

Interesting. In every detective novel I've ever read the number one suspect is always the person that finds the body.

Fiona moves closer to him. "Why do you say that?"

He drops a wrench and a dirty rag onto the floor. "Because I knew Peter better than anyone. He was special. There was something magical about him."

This guy is either a lover or someone who wanted to be one. "So, you don't believe the estate lawyer's explanation of his death."

"No way. That guy has been lying about everything. Peter never said anything about having a will, let alone an estate lawyer."

Fiona looks over at me and I nod. Definitely a former lover.

She puts her hand on his shoulder. "I'm very sorry for your loss, Mr. Jones, and I want you to know both my partner and I agree with you. Mr. Hamlyn was indeed murdered. Any clue who it might be? Did Peter have any enemies?"

I like how Fiona is not jumping to conclusions about Peter's partner.

The man fights back tears. "Peter was a marshmallow. Everyone who came to the restaurant loved him." He hesitated for a moment. "I loved him."

Mr. Jones clenched his fists. "There was a regular that always pushed him to do magic. He wasn't a bad person, just the most irritating guy on the planet."

Fiona nods and gets ready to take a note on her phone. "You wouldn't happen to know his name?"

"Harry Potter."

I try not to laugh. "His legal name."

Mr. Jones scoffs. "It is his legal name. He spells it Hairy Poter."

I can't help but burst out laughing. Mr. Jones sighs. "Yeah, some people are beyond fanatics."

Fiona somehow manages to keep a straight face. "Mr. Jones, I hope you don't mind me asking but were you and Peter partners? Did you live together?"

"We didn't live together, per se. I did stay over at his place a lot. We were pretty serious for over a year. I still have an apartment, so I could study late at night. I'm hoping to pass the bar by the end of the year."

The last thing I would guess was Mr. Jones was a dishwasher studying to be a lawyer. "Why the dishwasher gig?"

A tinge of red hits his cheeks. "I had a thing for Peter. I saw an ad for a dishwasher, and I thought what better way to get close to him."

The things love can drive us to do. "Smart move."

He breaks a tiny smile. "Yes, it worked out. Until

some psycho killed Peter. Have you talked to that lawyer? Something is fishy about him."

Fiona sighs. "He is evading us, which is surprising as it only makes him even more of a candidate." She looks at Mr. Jones frantically breaking down the dishwashing equipment. "Why are you helping the lawyer if you are suspicious of him?"

Jones picks up the wrench he threw on the floor. "I don't get my last paycheck unless I do what he says."

The lawyer is a real piece of work. "No wonder you don't like him."

Jones' stranglchold of the wrench says it all. "I better get back to work." He turns to Fiona. "If I were you, I'd chase the lawyer down. If he even is a lawyer."

Fiona's perfectly arched brows furrow. "What do you mean?"

"I can't say for certain as I never talked to him myself, which if you ask me is on purpose. If what Shelly the hostess told me is true about Peter's supposed will, the lawyer doesn't know what he's talking about. I've studied estate law for the bar, and that guy is full of it."

With that revelation, we head back to the car. I sit in the Beemer wondering who the lawyer guy really is. I turn to Fiona, "So what do you think of Jones's big lawyer revelation?"

"I think Mr. Jones is right. The lawyer is hiding something for certain."

Starting up the engine, I put the address of the lawyer into my GPS. "Let's see if we can catch him at homc."

Fiona smiles and holds up her hand. "Fingers crossed."

As I steer the car toward Malibu, I wonder what estate lawyer makes the kind of money to afford to live in such an exclusive beach community. Part of me wishes for my sidekick. In fact, the urge to get him becomes overwhelming. "Hey, do you mind if I pick up Holmes? He could do some reconnaissance for us. Find out if the guy is home or not."

She stops scrolling through her phone. "Having another set of eyes can't hurt,"

As I turn and pick up the Santa Monica freeway, I realize Fiona will see my tiny bungalow and think I'm a total loser wizard. She wouldn't know that my nine-hundred-and-fifty-foot bungalow a block from the beach cost me every dime I saved. In today's market it could easily go for two million dollars. I had a hard enough time coming up with the fifty thousand down payment. Could I have conjured money? Sure. But doing so I would have broken a major rule of the Twelfth Order.

I try not to be self-conscious as I pop off the freeway and head toward my street. Pulling into my small one car driveway I say, "This is my tiny abode."

Fiona opens the passenger door and steps out before I can catch her. She breathes in deep. "The smell of salt in the air. You must be close to the ocean."

"Yes, it's only a block away. Would you like to see it?"

She shakes her head. "No, although it is tempting. Let's pick up Holmes and see if we can get lucky."

Maybe she is being polite. Even someone from London knows that Malibu is prime ocean real estate—not Santa Monica.

I put the key in the door and face my canine sidekick. Holmes looks up at me with his sad brown eyes. "It is about time you rescue me from my boredom."

Talk about pouring on the guilt. I pat him on the head. "Sorry, Holmes, but you can't be with me all the time."

Fiona stands between the dog and me as if she expects a fight. "We thought you'd love a trip to the beach."

Holmes thrusts his nose up toward the ceiling. "The beach is a block away. I've seen it."

Talk about a tough crowd. "You haven't seen Malibu beach."

His floppy ears perk up. "Do you mean the beach of the stars?"

Fiona chuckles. "I do believe so. Who do you want to see Halle Berry or Robert Downey Jr.?"

How does she know they live there? Is she secretly hiding a Malibu star homes map?

Holmes makes a chuffing noise. "Actually, I would prefer to meet Cher."

Fiona and I look at each other and burst out laughing.

Holmes barks loudly. "I don't see what is so amusing. Cher is an icon."

I stop laughing. "That she is. Sorry for laughing, but I thought you would have named a different icon, like Jack Nicolson."

He shakes his head. "He's a good actor, but Cher truly commands a room."

Fiona stops chuckling. "That is true. I met her once. She is larger than life."

Holmes shifts in the back seat. "You really met her?"

"Yes, at the BAFTA awards. I was there with a friend."

Fiona seems to run in a far different circle than I do. "Okay, enough about celebrities. Let's concentrate on nailing the supposed lawyer."

The rest of the ride to Malibu is silent except for the occasional sound of Fiona texting someone and Holmes muttering to himself as he looks out the window.

The Pacific Coast Highway is a bit backed up as we make our way to the prime section of Malibu where the homes run along the cliffs overlooking the beach.

Fiona looks up from her phone. "Ms. Burke has confirmed that the lawyer is back home and alone. Except for his Doberman." She turns to face Holmes. "You can take care of him, can't you?"

Holmes stops slobbering all over my back window. "Of course, I can. I have a size advantage."

Fiona leans toward Holmes. "Not much of one. The Doberman is more agile."

This is going to turn into a major feud if I don't stop it. "Holmes has a weight advantage. I've seen him wrestle another dog he's good." A little white lie to defend my sidekick shouldn't get me in too much trouble.

Holmes thrusts one of his large ears in Fiona's direction. "These are one of my best weapons."

Fiona could take advantage of such an opening, but she just smiles. "I bet. You can easily suffocate someone with those ears."

Happy I managed to stop a feud between my partner and my sidekick, now I face the impossible task of finding a place to park near the house. After driving past once I realize I'm going to have to use a bit of magic. I snap my fingers and a space appears just large enough to park my car two houses to the north of the lawyer's house.

As I carefully maneuver the Beemer into the spot, Fiona claps lightly. "A very nice bit of magic."

I try to act innocent knowing we aren't supposed to use magic. "What are you talking about? I just missed the spot the first time we drove past."

Holmes nudges my shoulder with his huge muzzle. "You're right. I saw it too."

Fiona chuckles. "All right boys, it's not nice to team up against a woman."

I open my door, making sure of my footing as the small cliff I filled with magic dirt is only four inches wider than my car. Moving quickly along the road I make it to the passenger side of the car just as Fiona opens the door for herself and Holmes. I give her a slight bow and guide her to the street. In my best BBC broadcaster voice, I say, "We will do our best to oblige you, madam." I turn to Holmes. "Isn't that right Holmes?"

He nudges my hand. "That is a poor imitation of

my voice, sir."

Fiona pats Holmes on the head. "I agree. Now Holmes remember you must act as any normal dog would. Absolutely no talking."

He nods and trots in front of her. Holmes sniffs the perimeter of the house that faces nothing but the beach and the sea. He sits next to the front door motioning as if to give us the all clear. Maybe Ms. Burke had it wrong about the lawyer having a Doberman.

Fiona leans over and whispers in my ear. "Let me take the lead."

The warmth of her breath makes my ear tingle. Despite my reaction, I can do nothing but nod. We approach the door, and a camera's red light begins to blink frantically. I place my hands behind my back and silence the alarm. Next, I disable the camera hovering over our heads and unlock the door. In cases like this I think a bit of simple magic isn't totally breaking the rules. I motion for Fiona to open the door. With amazing skill, she walks across the marble entry in her high heels without making a sound. Holmes remains outside, waiting for the Doberman to appear.

We move into the main part of the house and take in the wall-to-wall windows looking out at the ocean. On the large sectional sofa facing the view sits a bald man peering out at the waves.

Without turning around, he says, "I assume you have a search warrant, or you are breaking and entering."

Fiona strides around the sofa and blocks his view.

"You've been avoiding us, Mr. Russel. That should be reason enough."

Ms. Burke must have supplied a name along with the address. I join Fiona. "We have found no evidence that Peter Hamlyn had a will, let alone an estate attorney.

Then Mr. Russel looks me straight in the face. "I may have lied about what kind of lawyer I am, but you are barking up the wrong tree if you think I have anything to do with Hamlyn's death. I was hired to procure the restaurant for my client, nothing more."

My gut has no reaction to his words. It seems to have taken the Switzerland position.

I glance over at Fiona as she rolls her eyes at the lawyer. "Thou doth protest too much."

Obviously, her gut thinks he's at least in the running.

Hearing the sound of the alarm beeping, Mr. Russel breaks into a satisfied grin which is slightly lopsided. It seems my magic didn't cut the alarm signal in time.

As we get ready to flee, Holmes races into the living room and jumps up onto Mr. Russel's lap. With the Doberman noticeably absent, Holmes wrestles the lawyer to the ground. Then he sticks his muzzle in his pocket and pulls out a piece of paper. Mr. Russel stares up at Fiona, who is aims a small caliber weapon straight at him.

Holmes trots over to me and nudges my hand. I take the paper and open it up. My eyes grow wide when I read what it says. "Part one of the plan is complete. Now on to part two."

THE MYSTERY MAN

The pain of teeth sinking into flesh takes a minute to register, as I look down and see the Doberman has his mouth clenched around my wrist. Holmes leaps to my defense and jumps onto the back of the Doberman. He copies the Doberman's led and sinks his teeth into the dog's neck.

Fiona shouts out, "Call off your dog." She moves the muzzle of the gun until it is touching the lawyer's forehead, "Now!"

He claps his hand and signals down. "Stop, Manfred."

The Doberman reluctantly lets go of my wrist that is weeping blood from the puncture wounds the teeth have left behind. As soon as I get outside, I need to cast a healing spell. The incisor teeth marks are deep. I take the opportunity to drip blood all over the lawyer's pure white sectional. He grits his teeth but does nothing with a gun still pointed at his head. I lead Holmes outside when I notice he too is wounded.

I hear a loud clanking sound and then Fiona appears. She looks down at my wrist, which is no longer bleeding. "I see you've healed yourself." She looks over at Holmes. "Did you get hurt?"

He shakes his head. "No, I'm fine." He coughs up an object. "Just swallowed a tuft of the Doberman's fur."

My eyes drift to Fiona's left hand that is red and swollen. "What happened to you?"

She gives me a wry smile. "I might have punched the lawyer out."

I take her hand in mine. "Let me take care of your pain."

She pulls her hand away. "It is well earned. If it gets worse, I'll let you know. Now let's get the note back to WI-6 for analysis."

Holmes sticks his snout in my hand that is holding the paper. "Strange. The paper has no odor."

I look down at the note and know it holds far more mysteries.

❦

THE PIT IS BUZZING WITH ACTIVITY AS USUAL. WE move through the darkness to the back of the room to report into Mr. Pierre. I stop by my assigned desk. "Holmes. You can wait here. I have no idea how long our meeting will last, and I don't want you to get bored. You can take a nap while you wait."

Holmes looks up at me with what can only be

described as a smile. "How thoughtful of you. After all the excitement in Malibu, I could use one."

Fiona pats his head. "You did a wonderful job. You deserve a rest."

As Holmes curls up by the desk, Fiona and I move to the back of *The Pit* to Mr. Pierre's domain. We are greeted by an empty desk. I shrug my shoulders as we stand, waiting for our boss to materialize. A blast of fragrance like a giant peony air freshener exploded signals Mr. Pierre's arrival.

He looks up from behind his desk as he smooths his mustache to pointed perfection. "Ms. Burke said you discovered something at the lawyer's residence. What is it?"

I lean over the desk and hand him the folded paper. His eyes narrow as he reads the note. "This is an interesting development." He signals Ms. Burke, who races over to his side.

"Sir?"

He hands her the paper. "Take this to the lab and have it analyzed. I want a complete breakdown in ten minutes."

She nods her head and takes off into the darkness of *The Pit*. In a normal detective story, the analysis of evidence can take days if not weeks. In the wizard world ten minutes is like a week. Mr. Pierre motions for us to sit down as two chairs appear behind us. I smile when I see they are the infamous plastic lawn chairs from my first interview. Hopefully Mr. Pierre isn't expecting this to be a long visit.

"Mr. Dunne, what does your gut tell you about the suspect you interviewed today?"

Coming from Mr. Pierre I know it is a loaded question. "Sir, my gut took the Switzerland position."

He turns toward my partner. "And you Ms. Singh?"

"I think the lawyer is guilty of some major crimes... murder however... I'm not certain."

He smiles and strokes his mustache like a beloved pet. "I am glad both of you are being reserved in your judgment. It is always desirable to hold your opinions about a suspect until you have absolute proof of their guilt."

I feel bad Fiona is getting schooled because of being partnered up with me. But as I look at the serene expression on her face, she shows no sign of anger. The expression on her face can only be called meditative. Maybe she has transported herself to another place in her mind. I wouldn't blame her.

"What do you think the paper means, Mr. Dunne?"

I lean back in my chair and wish I hadn't as a piercing pain hits my back from the hard plastic slats. "I believe one could guess by the note that plan one is complete. I would think plan one was either arranging the death of Mr. Hamlyn, or the procurement of the restaurant for his client."

Fiona's facial expression changes to one of pride in her partner.

"The later, I'm certain. Someone of the lawyer's personality type would never be directly involved in anything as sloppy as murder."

Ms. Burke returns with the note. She places it on

Mr. Pierre's desk and taps on his computer screen. "Sir, here are the results of the analysis." She points to something on the screen. "I thought this was interesting."

Mr. Pierre's eyes hover over the image. He looks up at us, his eyes twinkling. "The results from the lab are quite curious. There were notes written on the paper in invisible ink."

Fiona leans forward. "Really? I didn't think anyone one did that sort of thing anymore."

I must admit I'm as surprised as she is.

Mr. Pierre continues. "The scribbles in the margin of the note in invisible ink make it quite clear that Mr. Dunne's gut is correct on what plan one's goal was. The lawyer was directed to acquire Peter's restaurant space. There is nothing about doing it by nefarious means, however."

So, my gut was right about one thing. "Sir, should we assume that is correct?"

"Not necessarily." He looks back at the computer screen. "The lab also discovered another disappearing ink message was used, but they were unable to decipher it. They used several spells and incantations but have been unable to decipher it so far. The ink seems to be made from ancient ingredients."

Fiona uncrosses her legs and sits up at attention as if a general just walked into the room. "We had a similar ink pop up in one of our mysterious deaths." Fiona inches her chair closer to Mr. Pierre. "Sir, my gut tells me somehow these mysterious deaths were related."

He nods and takes a sip of coffee from a bright yellow cup that materialized on the corner of his desk. "This is our first unusual death. How many have you had in London?"

"They were not unusual in the same sense as Peter's. But the circumstances were odd. One wizard was killed while walking his dog. The long lead somehow became tangled around his neck."

My stomach gets a bit queasy imagining how a dog could strangle his owner. "And you could find no one who might have used the leash to murder the wizard?"

She sighs. "No. As unlikely as it seems, we could find no person who was responsible. All clues signaled it was the dog."

Mr. Pierre twirls the left side of his mustache. "Quite disconcerting."

Holmes would never do anything like that to me would he?

Ms. Burke strolls back over to the desk with a satisfied grin on her face. "I've located the infamous Hairy Poter." She hands me a piece of paper. I find the fact that they deliver information in such an old-fashioned way quite charming. It also is far less violating then the Twelfth Order's wizards' habit of entering people's minds.

"You'll find Hairy's address and phone number on the note. I'm sure he will be quite excited to talk to you." She leans over my shoulder seductively and whispers in my ear. "You should have him eating out of your hand. He's a big TV detective show fan."

Mr. Pierre clears his throat a bit too loudly. "DS,

please report back bright and early tomorrow morning with your latest update on the case."

Fiona gets up and strides through *The Pit* like she is on a runway garnering quite the obvious male admiration from Ross and Smith. I catch up with her in the hallway. "Guess you are in one big hurry to meet Hairy Poter."

She doesn't laugh. "Why do men have to leer at me?"

Spoken like a woman who has no idea how strikingly beautiful she is. Not that that excuses my male counterparts' behavior. "I'm sorry, but some of the male species haven't evolved much past Cro-Magnon stage."

She finally cracks a smile. "You're right. I swear one of them was going to grab my hair and drag me into the deepest darkest depths of *The Pit* wearing a fur outfit and carrying a club."

I laugh. "I can totally see Ross doing that."

She touches my shoulder. "I think you have an admirer too. Ms. Burke literally was breathing down your neck."

A snuffling sound comes from behind me. "Did you forget something?"

I look down at Holmes knowing I'd done exactly what he accused me of. "Yes, I did sorry, Holmes. The pressure of the case is getting to me."

He looks up at me with his sad doggie brown eyes and I know my apology was not accepted.

Fiona pats Holmes on the head. "I'm at fault too. You may not be my sidekick, but I forgot we left you by the desk as well."

Holmes shakes his body like he has been given a bath. "That's enough ass kissing. Don't we have a case to solve?"

❧

DRIVING TO KOREATOWN, ONE THING BECAME CLEAR about Hairy and his apartment location on the south side of town. He definitely had a tight housing budget. The area where his apartment is located is not one of the better neighborhoods of Los Angeles, although the food choices are excellent.

Fiona pulls her phone out of her purse. "Let me call him. I think he will respond better to a British voice considering his name choice."

Holmes snuffles. "I cannot wait to meet the fellow that would name himself after a character in a book."

For some reason I feel a bit indignant by Holmes' comment. "He was a powerful wizard. What's wrong with that?"

Fiona puts her long red lacquered nail to her lips. "Quiet down, chaps." She punches in the fictional wizard fans phone number. Then she puts the call on speaker phone. His voice message is exactly what I expected. In a childlike high squeaky male voice he says, "This is the honorable Hairy Poter speaking. I'm too busy casting spells to answer the phone. Leave a message and I may or may not get back to you."

"This is Ms. Singh of the Dumbledoor Detective Agency. I would like to..."

The sound of static rings out of her phone and a garbled voice says, "Hello, can I help you?"

Fiona purrs. "Yes, you can, Mr. Poter. I would like to speak with you about Peter Hamlyn. I heard you were a regular at the Health Nut. Are you free now?"

More garbled noises. "Umm, if it's important." He gives her the address to his apartment. "See you soon."

As he clicks off, I can't help but laugh at the fact we already know where Hairy lives, and that Fiona's charms never fail her. "You sure know how to give good phone."

Fiona's brow furrows. "What do you mean?"

"You sounded very British and quite sexy. Great name of the agency too."

She gives me a slight smile. "We detectives have to use all our skills to get suspects to cooperate."

Holmes stops drooling all over my window and turns to Fiona. "I believe they are called feminine wiles."

Before I can make a snappy retort my screen buzzes. An unknown number pops up on the screen, but I pick up anyway in case it's an old Zoomer client. "You've reached Derrick Dunne."

A frantic voice booms through the car speakers. "Mr. Dunne it's Mr. Jones, Peter's..."

"Yes, I remember your name. You sound out of breath. What is wrong?"

"You told me to call if I remembered anything and I have. There was this guy who came into the restaurant one day about a month ago and spoke to Peter. I can't really describe the man as he looked so ordinary.

Nothing about him stands out in my mind. Average build, average face, and mousy brown hair."

The first thing I think of is detective Smith. "Yes. I know what you mean, an everyman."

A sound of relief fills Jones's voice. "Yes, that's it exactly. Anyway, when Peter came back from talking to him outside in the alley, he seemed very agitated. I asked him what was wrong, but all he would say was a person from his past came back to haunt him." He takes a deep breath. "I'm sorry it didn't come to me sooner. You see, I never saw the guy come to the restaurant again. Peter didn't mention him again after that one encounter."

"That's good information. Thank you for calling."

Jones doesn't hang up. "I had a weird feeling about him, but then I just forgot about it. That is until I saw someone similar today."

Fiona squeezes my hand and whispers. "This could be an important lead."

I nod. "Thanks again, Mr. Jones. We will see if we can find out who he is."

Fiona points to the GPS on her phone reminding me we need to get to Hairy Poter's apartment. "Something tells me things are going to start falling in place from now on."

I smile as the first good omen comes into view. A parking place directly in front of the apartment.

Fiona's gazes up and down the block filled with older five and ten story brick apartments. "Do you think it is wise to park your car here? This neighborhood looks quite dangerous." She eyes a group of scruffy guys three apartments down. "Those men are practically drooling over your BMW."

Holmes growls in their direction. "She's right. The second we leave the car they are going to steal it, the tire rims, or both."

"Please don't worry. I'm a wizard, remember? I'll put a protection spell on the car."

Fiona turns and eyes Holmes. "It is your duty to protect your owner's property."

Holmes thrusts out his chest. "Ms. Singh, are you implying I would shirk my duty?"

They sure know how to rub each other the wrong way. "Guys, calm down. How about I leave Holmes in the car and cast the protection spell?" Holmes gets ready to protest and I hold up my hand. "The spell will protect you as well."

Holmes sits back on his hunches. "Fine."

I mutter the protection spell under my breath and get out of the car. Staring down the group of guys, at least I don't see any signs they are in a gang. I race over and open the door for Fiona. The whistles and hoots start before she is even totally out of the car. We walk quickly up to the front door. I push the buzzer for 308. Nothing happens. Snapping my fingers, the door pops open.

Fiona steps inside quickly and I follow right behind her. The inside of the apartment building smells like a combination of pizza, Asian food, and cheap household cleaner. I push the button for the elevator and realize too late it had gum stuck to it.

Fiona's nose crinkles. "This place is charming, isn't it?"

I conjure a napkin and wipe the gum residue off my finger. "Oh, yes. Full of wonderful amenities like free gum."

We chuckle the whole ride to the third floor. We exit the elevator and stand on a carpet so old and dirty it is hard to tell what the original color was. As we walk halfway down the hallway, we discover apartment 308. Fiona rings the bell, and the door creaks open revealing a short, stocky, pimple faced blond male about twenty years old. Far different then the character he idolizes except for his height.

He eyes Fiona and smiles. "Are you the wonderful British woman from the Dumbledoor Detective Agency?"

She beams. "Yes, I am. May we come in and ask you a few questions?"

"We?" He frowns and looks past her to see my smiling face. "Okay." He reluctantly opens the door just wide enough for us to get inside his apartment.

After the smells of the lobby, I expected his apartment to be strewn with empty pizza boxes and Korean take out containers—the typical young male bachelor pad. Instead, we entered an apartment that smells of orange peel air freshener. The living space is a nicely appointed studio dominated by a grey couch, a fur throw and two striped decorative pillows. Next to it stands a comfy looking black leather club chair. They both faced an enormous 72" TV on a low wood stand.

The kid must make a decent living doing something besides playing video games like I thought.

Fiona sits down on the club chair relieved it isn't the stained mess she seemed to have imagined. I sit down on the far end of the sofa. "Nice place you have here, Hairy."

He ignores me and hovers over Fiona. "Would you like anything to drink? I have sparkling water, orange juice, and... tea." He slaps his forehead. "I have a very nice oolong. Hold on a moment."

Before she can say a word, he races over to the well-appointed kitchenette along the left wall. As he busies himself preparing the tea, I wish I could pop into Fiona's mind and go over our interview plan. The idea is tempting but I think she would take it as the ulti-mate violation. Instead, I pretend I'm back in grade school and conjure paper and pen to write her a note. "I'll let you take the lead in this one but if I tap my foot, I have a question I want to ask him"

I crumple up the paper and toss it to her. She catches it with the ease of a pro baseball player. The whole thing goes unnoticed as Hairy stands to the cooktop watching over the tea kettle, waiting for it to get to the right temperature. Then he places several spoonful's of leaf tea in a silver infuser.

Fiona coughs to cover the sound of her uncrum-pling the paper. She reads it and nods. I give her a thumbs up as Hairy carries out a black tray containing a small white china teapot with a matching cup of tea and sugar and creamer. He places it on the small side table next to the club chair. "I hope you will find the tea to your liking."

I try not to laugh at his forced British accent.

Fiona waits a minute before she pours her tea. Then she places a sugar cube in her simple china cup and a splash of milk from a small pitcher on the tray. The whole thing seems quite civilized, like something out of a BBC TV show.

Fiona takes a sip and smiles broadly at Hairy as he sits on the opposite side of the sofa like I have a contagious disease. "It has a wonderful flavor. I believe it is Twining's. Is it not?"

Now I've slipped into a historical film.

Hairy puffs out his chest just a bit. "It is. I'm so glad you recognized the company. It's the only oolong I'll let touch my lips."

Fiona takes another sip and then places her white china cup back on the black metal tray. "Mr. Poter, we'd like to ask you a few questions. The first, why did you choose to be a regular at the Health Nut?" She eyes his small pot belly.

Hairy is too enamored with Fiona to realize he's been insulted.

"The smoothies from the juice bar were really good. But the main reason was Peter's magic. His sleight of hand was amazing. I never could figure out how he did it."

Of course, he couldn't because Peter used real magic.

Fiona nods. "Yes, I heard he was quite good. "Did

you ever see Peter have a problem with any of the guests at the restaurant?"

Hairy rubs his chin back and forth as if it could conjure up a memory. "Well, he did have to throw one guy out. He was taking seconds at the juice bar. And there was a time when a girl was harassing one of the guy regulars." He cracks a smile. "She was really into him. He looked like Kit Harrington."

Here I thought *Game of Thrones* was so yesterday.

Fiona nods. "Did you hear anyone talk about Peter and Jones being together?"

Hairy chuckles. "Everyone knew about them. When they closed up the restaurant every night it was obvious that they had a thing going on."

Fiona nods. "Did anyone ever seem annoyed or jealous they were together?"

I have no idea where she is going with the questioning. Peter's murder did not seem like a crime of passion.

Hairy rubs his chin again. "There was one regular guy who had a thing for Peter, but he never got anywhere. Peter was polite to him but that was it. Have you seen Jones? Can't imagine anyone could be more handsome."

He was good looking for sure, but I've seen handsomer men. I tap my foot on the carpeted floor loud enough for Fiona to hear. She gives me a hand signal that she is turning the questioning over to me. "Hairy, we've taken up quite a bit of your time. I have one last question for you. Did you ever notice a man who came into the restaurant who looked very ordinary? Another person we interviewed said the man asked to see Peter. He seemed a bit agitated."

Hairy didn't need to rub his chin this time. "Oh yes, I remember him. He came in the restaurant about a month ago. He was very nondescript, yet I remember him. There was some rage brewing inside the man just under the surface. It made me feel uneasy. He really stood out because most of the people who came into the Health Nut were very mellow."

I nod having been there and seen the restaurant's vibe. "Can you describe the man for me?"

Hairy's brow furrows as he thinks hard. "You know he is hard to describe. He was just so average. Nothing about him stood out."

It hits me like a shot why both Hairy and Jones can't describe the man. He used an identity-cloaking spell. The mystery man is a wizard.

9

———

HIDDEN SECRETS

You would think the revelation that our mystery man is a wizard would get us closer to solving the case. You'd be wrong. Wizards are terrible at sensing the evil in each other. I learned that lesson early on in my wizard career. After only three months on my Zoomer reconnaissance job, I ran across a Ronin wizard. They are rogue wizards who became mercenaries working for other paranormals that want nothing less than to take over the world.

On a bright sunny day in LA during my first year of Zoomer driving, I picked up an ordinary looking wizard. With my meager newbie mind reading skills, I could not detect which Order he was from. I had no idea picking him up on the corner of Pico and La Brea would be my first paranormal life lesson. Due to my innocence, the wizard suckered me into helping him deceive a man who I thought he was helping. What seemed like a friend rescuing a friend was a kidnapping that I aided and abetted. This mistake sticks with me even to this day. My fairytale vision of wizard's only doing good in the world was dashed forever. I had the same feeling at the age of five when my best friend broke the news that Santa Claus wasn't real.

I'm going to need to rely on Fiona and Holmes when we find and confront the wizard suspect. My gut is useless to me when it comes reading my fellow wizards.

Fiona squeezes my arm as we head back to our desks. "You seem devastated by the news that our mystery man is a wizard."

I nod and plop down in my chair. "I've confronted an evil contemporary before. It changed my life."

Holmes looks up at me with surprise. "That is quite the dramatic statement. People, including paranormals, let you down every day."

Fiona smiles. "Holmes seems to be a philosopher. You forget one thing, Mr. Dunne."

I laugh. "You just noticed."

She doesn't laugh. "We don't know if the wizard in question has anything to do with Mr. Hamlyn's death. They could have had some grievance that was later resolved. A good detective never jumps to conclusions. Maybe the experience in your past needs to be set aside in this case."

I know she is right. It is one of Mr. Bullock's tenants to not jump to conclusions. I let out a deep yoga breath. "I promise I will take your words to heart."

Holmes snuffles. "It's wonderful to see partners play nice in the sandbox."

I wonder if Mr. Bullock conjures key phrases in Holmes's brain like you would program a robot. Somehow, I can't get away from the science fiction analogy. A message pops up on my computer screen. It's from Fiona. "I sent a request for the security footage at the restaurant for last month's recordings to be sent to us. We might get lucky and find a clip of our mystery wizard."

I message her back. "Perfect. Sometimes identity magic doesn't translate to video. I've solved two assignments that way. Can I ask why you are messaging me rather than us just having a conversation?"

"Because Mr. Smith is a wizard who poses as an everyman too."

Due to Fiona's revelation about Smith, we agree to watch the security footage at my place. Fiona pulls a dining chair next to me as I open my laptop on the dining room table that doubles as my desk. Shalimar tickles at my nose and I breathe in a little deeper enjoying the closeness to Fiona. She seems not to feel any attraction to me at all. But the more time I spend with her I feel a pull of chemistry. It takes me by surprise as I thought that part of my life had completely shut down after Tara's death.

I click on the video file and slowly scroll through hours of footage. After an hour of watching customers go in and out of the Health Nut, the mystery wizard remains elusive.

Fiona gets up and stretches her long legs. "Do you mind if we take a break? I'm a bit peckish. Are there any good restaurants nearby?"

Holmes races toward the front door. "Brilliant. I need some exercise and to breathe the salt air."

Having an early dinner with Fiona sounds like a dangerous prospect considering my growing feelings toward her. But with her obvious lack of interest in me, I have nothing to fear. Holmes coming along on the other hand is a far bigger problem. I stare down at him as he gazes longingly at his leash. "You must promise not to run off, and most of all not to talk."

He huffs. "You insult my intelligence. I know how to behave in public."

Fiona pulls out her phone and checks her messages. I wonder if she has someone special back in London. Of course, she does. She's amazing.

Fiona stashes her phone back in her purse looking just a bit disappointed. "Do you have a favorite restaurant? I'd love someplace with an ocean view. I haven't had much of a chance to sightsee."

I beam knowing the perfect spot. "There is an incredible restaurant overlooking the ocean in the Hotel Miramar. It has a quintessential beachy vibe."

She loops her arm around mine. "Lead the way."

Holmes barks and paws at his leash. "Don't forget about me."

Fiona pats him on his rump. "Hard to do that, big boy."

I gently take Fiona's hand off my arm. "I better do as he says, or we'll never hear the end of it."

Holmes sticks his large black nose up in the air as I pull his leash down. "You know I'm standing right here."

Fiona gives me a wink as I take her arm and we step out the door with Holmes. I click the digital lock on my front door and head down the street toward the ocean. "Luckily it's just a quick walk to the restaurant. I can hear your stomach growling."

Fiona squeezes my hand knowing I'm teasing. "I'm famished."

With Holmes striding before us pulling hard on his leash, his nose twitching back and forth taking in all the amazing combination of smells found at the beach. Everything from suntan lotion, to beer, to the salty sea air tickle at his nose.

Fiona takes in the sights of the people strolling by some wearing hardly anything. I wonder if it will offend her British sensibilities.

She whispers as a ripped man in his early twenties wearing a turquoise thong topped off by a spiked blond head of hair passes by. "I think he has a wonderful body, except in one location."

I laugh. "You have a keen eye."

"We detectives notice those kinds of things."

It's wonderful to have a moment of fun with Fiona after a few action-packed days together. "Of course. Right down to the tiniest details."

She throws back her hair and laughs with a freedom I haven't seen from her before. I lead her and Holmes down a walkway to the Miramar Hotel. "Usually, you would need a reservation because it's a popular spot, but I dine here quite a lot so I'm a regular."

As we enter the hotel, Fiona takes in the quintessential beach decor with its use of ocean blue stripes, ikat fabrics, and rattan furniture. The hotel has an elegant yet casual style. We walk up the restaurant's entrance and Fiona sucks in a breath when she sees the endless view of the pale sand beach and the ocean beyond.

The white clad hostess eyes Holmes. "Small dogs are allowed, but not horses."

The endless palm trees that frame the view are also the perfect place to tie up Holmes. He glares at me as I lead him outside the restaurant and toward a patch of small fan palms.

He mutters under his breath. "That hostess is prejudiced against big dogs. It is patently unfair."

I pat him on the head and tie him to a palm tree where I can keep an eye on him from inside the restaurant. I whisper near his big floppy ear. "Behave yourself. No Labradoodle chasing."

He huffs. "Doodles are a silly dog craze. I much prefer the long silky locks of an Afghan hound."

I nod, knowing they do have beautiful long fur that sometimes is mistaken for a woman's hair. "Yes, they are very pretty dogs." I tap him on his large shoulders. "Relax. Enjoy the smells and the sights. Just not too much."

I feel a bit guilty leaving him all alone. He is a handsome dog that someone might want to steal, so I cast a protection spell around him just in case. If anyone tries to untie him, they are going to get a jolt of electricity as strong as one from a Taser.

The hostess makes a note of the fact I'm now dogless and leads me over to a less than desirable table. I notice Stacey, my favorite waitress, nearby and signal her.

She bounds over, her red curls bouncing on her shoulders. "Hey, Derrick. It's been a while. How have you been?" She eyes Fiona. "Is she the reason you haven't been here in a week?"

I feel Fiona tense up next to me. "No, Stacey. I started a new job."

At this point the hostess gives up trying to seat us and hands the menus to Stacey. She smiles. "Ah, so you finally got tired of being a Zoomer driver." Stacey leads us to an amazing table with a hundred and eighty-degree view of the ocean. "Here you go. Best seat in the house. Enjoy."

Fiona raises an eyebrow as Stacey saunters off. "She seems to know you quite well."

I give her a crooked smile. "I won't divulge how well. It would be impolite."

Fiona chuckles. "No judgments from me. You are a handsome man; it is understandable you would enjoy playing the field."

It's nice to know she thinks I'm attractive. But she would never believe that I'm not a player after Stacey's performance. Not like I've had the time or the desire for an action-packed love life. Time to change the subject. I look down at the menu.

"My favorites for dinner are the roasted beet salad and the prosciutto and arugula pizza. If you have a large appetite, they have a lobster roll that is heaven. For dessert, the blueberry tiramisu is quite nice, but if you love chocolate, which I must confess that I do, the house made chocolate brownie with Tahitian vanilla gelato is the best I've ever had."

Fiona smiles as she peruses the menu. "Nice job changing the subject to food. Especially when you know I'm famished." She flips her menu over. "I will take your recommendations to heart. Especially the dessert. I'm what you Americans call a chocoholic."

"What do you call them in the UK?"

"Smart."

I laugh. "Touché."

Stacey flounces over all smiles. "So, what will it be, Derrick?"

I glance over at Fiona. "Ladies first."

Stacey leans a bit closer to Fiona. "What will you have?"

My partner smiles up at Stacey, ignoring her closeness. "Are there any chef specials?"

Stacey nods. "Yes, there are, but first I just want to say you have the coolest accent."

Fiona smiles but says nothing.

"Right," Stacey seems a bit flustered. "Today the chef specials are a filet of sole in a light wine sauce, and a mushroom risotto."

Fiona nods. "I'll have a beet salad and the sole."

Stacey doesn't need to write her order down. She

has an impressive memory. "Derrick? You want the usual?"

"I think I'll change it up today. I'll have the mushroom risotto and we'll split a brownie for dessert."

Stacey eyes Fiona" You must be pretty special for Derrick to share his brownie." Then she trounces off to put in our order.

Fiona has a curious look in her eyes. "It seems you are not the type of person who normally shares dessert. Interesting."

I lean back in the rattan chair, enjoying the support of the thick cushion. "Yes, I must confess, I'm terrible about sharing. Been that way since I was a kid."

Stacey returns with part of our order. She lays the beet salad between us assuming we will want to share. "The rest of your order should be out shortly."

Fiona picks up her fork and flips it over like most Europeans. She looks so cute eating the beets. They make her lips even redder as the juice hits her mouth. She puts down her fork, realizing I'm not eating but watching her. "I thought the beet salad was a favorite of yours. I'm happy to share. The portion is quite large."

I've embarrassed her. "Thank you. I didn't want to presume that because Stacey left an extra fork, I could dig in."

Fiona smiles and I can see her front teeth have a tinge of red. "Are you trying to prove you are better at sharing?"

There is an intimacy in her words. She is paying

attention to the tidbits I reveal about myself. I grace her with one of my crooked smiles. "How am I doing?"

She copies my expression perfectly. "Quite well."

Stacey arrives with my mushroom risotto and Fiona's sole. They both have been garnished to perfection.

Stacey turns to me as if Fiona isn't sitting at the same table. "Anything else I can get you Derrick? A glass of Pino?"

"No. I have to work tonight. I want to impress the new boss."

Stacey squeezes my shoulder then whispers in my ear. "You're wonderful at making good impressions."

Fiona finishes her mouthful of sole and narrows her eyes. "Are you still sticking to the story that you and Stacey have never dated?"

"Yes. We never really dated. Just hung out a bit."

Fiona chuckles. "You Americans are so caviler about sex."

I push my risotto around in my bowl a bit uncomfortable with the direction the conversation is going.

Thankfully Fiona must have remembered she is famished, as she digs into her beet salad with gusto. I take a bite of my risotto and we sit in silence eating our meals. Fiona is a patient detective. I put down my fork knowing she has won. "All right. I had a brief relationship with Stacey. Do you have a problem with that?"

Fiona sports a satisfied smile knowing she has got under my skin. Something it appears detectives' relish. "It really is none of my business. Sometimes I can't seem to take my detective hat off. Apologies."

Before I can tell her, my life is an open book, my phone buzzes, it's Stacey. "Hey, Derrick, you better go check on your dog. A sketchy looking guy is hovering around him."

I push back my chair. "I got a call that some guy is stalking Holmes. They are going to be in for a big surprise if they try to nab him.

Fiona gets up and then Stacey cuts her off. "Did you forget you ordered the brownie? Are you going to pay for your meal?"

Fiona sits back down. "You go. I'll settle the bill. Dinner is on me."

I give her a wink and head out the side door toward where I tied up Holmes. He is lying in the sun, totally ignoring a man with long blond hair wearing a blue T-shirt and board shorts hiding behind one of the palm trees. He doesn't look like a dog thief but then again, what do I know? Sensing he is about to make his move; I hang back a moment. Sure, enough he looks both ways and then darts for the leash tied to the tree. The second he touches it, the man is blasted by 50,000 volts. The electricity passes through his body, and he keels over and falls onto the sand.

Holmes turns his head and sniffs the air filled with ozone. I quickly move next to him. "Don't be alarmed. He isn't dead."

Holmes continues to sniff the air. "You better cover that up. Someone might recognize it."

I doubt we have much to fear as there is a gentle breeze, but I cast a spell to remedy the situation. Holding back a laugh, Holmes has a burst of flatulence.

The odor is so powerful the area suddenly smells like a sewer.

A delicate coughing sounds behind me. "What did you feed Holmes? That poor man has passed out."

I give her a devilish smile. "I used one of my favorite spells. It's called fart defense."

ONE MINUTE I'M TAKING FIONA BACK TO HER HOTEL after our lovely meal, the next I'm reversing course. I thought Zoomer drivers worked long hours. Detectives sure put in a lot of time as well. No night off as I hoped.

Staring at the screen in my car waiting to put in the address of our next suspect, Fiona squeezes my hand. "I just got a message from Ms. Burke. She went through the rest of the security tape and found the wizard. She also has two more possible suspects. The first is at two hundred fifty-seven La Brea Avenue, apartment three hundred and four."

I know that part of town well. Turning the wheel hard, I merge onto the freeway and head for the La Brea Avenue exit.

Fiona stares out the window. "It must feel slightly uncomfortable to be tracking down three suspects of your own kind."

I shrug my shoulders. "There is evil in any group of people, even magical ones."

We slow down almost as soon as we get on the San Diego freeway. We've hit the usual rush hour traffic.

"I've encountered rogue wizards before, just not ones that are serial killers. Most are all about power and showing off. Only once did one try to destroy Los Angeles. Some people would argue it would be no loss. Of course, I beg to differ."

Fiona stares out the window at the cars moving five miles an hour and the faint hint of brown in the air. "Parts of Los Angeles are not very attractive. I understand now why they call it the concrete jungle."

I nod. "Yes, all the pictures of palm trees and beaches don't really tell the whole story. Sections of Los Angeles are downright ugly."

"I always believed the Hollywood version. It's the one we were exposed to the most in the UK."

As I get off the La Brea off ramp, my nerves begin to prickle. I've never had to face an evil wizard before. Holmes seems oblivious to his owner's nerves as he sits in his usual position with his nose plastered to the window staring out at the endless cars.

Fiona pulls out her phone and scrolls through her messages. She seems disappointed at the lack of a certain message. How anyone could ignore such an amazing woman is beyond me.

She looks up from her phone and sighs. "People disappoint you every day."

"Sorry. I hope you don't mind me asking, but is it someone special?"

Fiona shifts in her seat and hangs her head down as if she has spotted something fascinating on the car carpet. "I thought so. Perhaps I was wrong."

I know the feeling. Someone I thought was the

perfect woman for me, turned out to be the exact opposite. She was the first and last woman who sensed something special about me, although I never once mentioned I was a wizard because it is strictly forbidden. One thing the woman didn't realize about dating a wizard, I had the power to wipe the memory of our relationship out of her mind. Stopped her fatal attraction syndrome right in its tracks. "I'm sorry. I haven't known you for very long, but you seem like an extraordinary woman inside and out."

She pushes a long strand of hair off her face. "Thank you. That is very kind."

Holmes puts his muzzle on her shoulder. "Any man who treats you badly does not deserve you."

Holmes and his movie quotes. I pull up in front of an unassuming older Spanish style apartment building. "He certainly isn't living in high style although I bet the apartment rents for well over twenty-five hundred dollars a month."

Fiona's mood brightens, grateful for a change in conversation. "The flats in London are double the price. The nicer parts of London have become more and more for the elite only."

I turn off the engine and get ready for a major hit to my debit card. The meters on the Westside are ridiculously pricey. "So, what is the plan?" I pull out my phone and look at the list of suspects again. "This Mr. Santos may have a few surprises up his sleeve if we try to break in. Wizards are notoriously paranoid."

Her brow furrows. "He might have the place rigged for explosives?"

I smile at the movie reference. "Usually, wizards are a bit more subtle."

She chuckles. "Got it. I'll be on alert."

I turn to face Holmes. "You need to stay here."

He huffs. "I'm supposed to guard the car, again? This doesn't look like a bad neighborhood."

"It's not. In case things get complicated, I'd rather I just have Fiona to worry about, not you too."

"Why not use my Bloodhound nose to your advantage? I can smell gun powder from quite a far distance."

Fiona pats his head. "I'm with you, Holmes. I think the more the merrier."

I get out of the car and open the back door. "Alright. I admit I've been outnumbered."

Holmes jumps down his tail wagging like gangbusters. "Your sidekick at the ready."

Our detective team of three approaches the apartment door, and I sigh when I see a keypad. "I'll take care of the door code. Holmes I'll let you off the leash so you can examine the perimeter of the building. The wizard might try to escape out the back. Be ready to take him down."

"My pleasure," he says before he trots down the side of the building his nose moving back and forth like an oscillating fan.

I lightly snap my fingers and the door opens. The lobby is surprisingly bland. Everything is beige, even the carpet. With no elevator in sight, we make our way up to the large staircase to the third floor. The beige carpeting continues down the hallway.

Fiona stands in front of apartment 304 and gives

me a signal. The hairs on my arms prickle when I sense magic inside. I close my eyes and concentrate on the door, and it pops open. We make our way into a sparsely furnished living room that is as boring as the lobby, only everything is white. I scan the perimeter of the room and a huge ball of magical light hurls toward me. Fiona instinctively pushes me aside as a strange white mist surrounds her. I blink twice as I watch her transform from a beautiful woman into a huge metal shield. The wizard's magic bounces off the shield and dissipates into the air. Within a minute the magical booby trap he laid for us is spent.

The white mist swirls around Fiona as she transforms back into human form. Her hair and clothing are flawless, like nothing ever happened. I stare at her wide-eyed, still having a hard time believing what I just saw.

She gives me a crooked smile. "I guess my secret is out. I'm a shifter."

10

INTERVIEW WITH A KILLER

Holmes walks around Fiona, sniffing her clothes like crazy. She taps him on the muzzle. "What are you smelling? Did some rancid magic hit me?"

Holmes shakes his head. "Not that I can tell. I want to know what a shifter smells like for the next time I come across one."

Fiona shrugs. "I hope my odor is not too offensive."

For a second, I wonder if that is why she wears a heavy perfume like Shalimar.

"Not at all." Holmes sniffs her again. "Your skin actually has a pleasant blend of sandalwood with a hint of night blooming jasmine."

I laugh. "Sounds like your sweat should be bottled up."

Fiona takes a magazine from Santos's coffee table and hurls it at me. "You're just mad I didn't tell you about my secret."

"A little. We are partners. We shouldn't have any

secrets between us. At least not really big ones. But then again, you probably saved my life, so I'll let it slide."

She beams. "Good. Because I had orders not to let you know unless it was an emergency."

Flashing back on the magical booby trap, I'm grateful for her skill. "Now I know, and I'm thankful."

Holmes stops smelling Fiona and trots over and paws at the door. "Enough wasting vital time chatting. Aren't there two more suspects on Ms. Burke's list?"

"Right." I open the door and Holmes hurries ahead of us making sure there are no other booby traps. As we make our way back to the car, I open the door for Fiona and lean in close breathing in her scent. All I smell is Shalimar. I guess I need to be a dog to smell her sandalwood and jasmine undertones.

Fiona tugs at my shirt collar. "Are you smelling me?"

I laugh and move slightly away from her. "After Holmes's description, I admit I became a bit curious."

She gives me a half smile. "And do I smell of my home country?'

I should have put it together sooner. Sandalwood and jasmine are distinctly Indian. "Alas, I only smell the Shalimar."

"That's too bad but I'm not surprised. Dogs have far more sensory receptors than we do. They can smell over ten thousand times better than humans."

Holmes moves next to me. "Actually, Bloodhounds can sense smell almost a hundred thousand times better than humans."

I open the back door for Holmes feeling a tad

jealous of his sensory skills. As I sit behind the wheel and start the engine, I can't help but laugh about being schooled by my partner and sidekick. "I guess you both are far more educated about a dog's sensory capacity than I am." I point to Fiona's phone. "So where to next?"

She scans Ms. Burke's message. "Six hundred and sixteen Nimes Road."

I take in a breath. "Are you sure? That's in a very pricey part of Bel Air."

Fiona's eyes narrow. "And how do you know that?"

I ponder whether I want to tell her the truth. Then I know I must after our big conversation about keeping secrets. "One of my Zoomer clients is a hot new model and I went with her to a party at a celebrity's house in Bel Air."

A crooked grin spreads across Fiona's lips. "First I find out about Stacey then you are telling me about another girl. And yet you say you don't play the field."

My shoulders tighten defensively. "Krissy and I are just friends. She's one of my regulars."

Holmes snorts. "Oh, is that what you call them these days?"

I take my hands off the wheel. "I surrender."

Fiona grabs the wheel as the car veers to the left. "We just are curious. Right Holmes?"

"Precisely."

I sigh and turn onto the San Diego Freeway headed south. "Not that you will believe me but as beautiful as Krissy is, I never once considered dating her."

Fiona doesn't look convinced. "Why? Was there too much competition?"

It's a low blow, but I take it in stride. "No, because she is a werewolf. They are way too high maintenance."

Fiona's musical laugh fills the car. "Now I understand. Krissy is double trouble."

I tap the steering wheel in agreement. "Exactly."

Holmes puts his muzzle on my shoulder. "She sounds like she would be a lot of fun."

Fiona nudges his muzzle off my shoulder. "Holmes. I thought you were civilized."

He sits back on his hunches. "I want my owner to stop moping around and find the right partner. Even if she's a damn wolf."

❧

AS WE DRIVE THROUGH THE GATES OF BEL AIR Fiona's eyes grow wide. "This is just like what I've seen on the telly back in the UK. The houses are as grand as a small palace."

"This is the section of Bel Air where all the old movie stars and directors lived. The likes of Marilyn Monroe, Tony Curtis, Alfred Hitchcock and more recent celebrities like Madonna and Nicolas Cage have all taken up residence."

Fiona laughs. "Why do I suddenly feel like I'm on a tour?"

I point to a house set back off the road. It has ivy growing over the front stucco façade and has an old-world Spanish feel. "That belonged to Nicolas Cage."

I slow down so Fiona can get a better look. "Funny, you wouldn't think a quirky actor like Nicolas, who loves to play eclectic roles, would like such a staid, old-world home."

I drive further down the road and turn left. "You'd be surprised. Would you have guessed I would live in a small Craftsman bungalow near the beach?"

"Touché" Fiona squeezes my arm. "No, I certainly would not. You seem much more the type of man who would live in a contemporary loft in a high rise downtown."

Interesting. It always amazes me how differently people perceive my personality. Krissy always teases me what a stick in the mud I am and how I act like an old man. Stacey thinks of me as a guy about town dating five women at once who goes surfing on the weekend. I guess my quirky personality can be interpreted many ways.

We finally arrive at Nimes Street. The house at six one six is set far back from the street high up on a knoll. A formidable wrought iron fence towers over the driveway entrance. As I pull closer, I see a pair of security cameras hovering over a keypad.

Fiona nudges my arm to stop the car. "It seems like Mr. Oppenheimer doesn't want unexpected visitors." She looks down at her message from Ms. Burke. "It says that from their surveillance of the residence, the suspect is home. I think I better call him up seeing all the precautions he has. You could use magic to get around his security but our surprise visit to Mr. Santos didn't turn out so well."

Holmes tears his nose away from the window. "What do you mean? We survived another day."

Fiona ignores his comment and dials a number. "Hello Mr. Oppenheimer, this is Ms. Teller. There is an issue I need to speak with you about...in person."

I can hear the beep of the message machine then a scrambling noise as if someone is frantically trying to pick something up. A thin male voice comes on the line. "Ms. Teller, this is Mr. Oppenheimer. I hope you are nearby. We need to get the photo shoot location locked down."

Fiona looks at me and shrugs. "Of course. We are approaching your driveway as we speak."

She nudges my arm off the center console. "We have the best luck. It appears he is expecting someone for a photo shoot. I'll try to sneak in a few questions about the restaurant. He must have gone there, or Ms. Burke wouldn't have put him on the list."

"Awesome idea." I open my console and pull out a pair of horn-rimmed glasses. Placing the glasses on my nose I turn to face Holmes. "What do you think? Do I look like a fancy New York photographer?

Holmes makes a muffling noise afraid to bark and call attention to the car. "The glasses look very GQ as a matter of fact."

Then I turn to Fiona holding up my phone. "Smile for the camera."

Fiona tries hard not to laugh. "Can I ask why you have a disguise stash in your console when you can conjure whatever you want?"

"Sometimes I don't have time, or there are too

many people around. The glasses are standard issue for reconnaissance duty. I have quite a few more props in the trunk. But I use the preppy glasses the most."

Holmes glances longingly back at the trunk. "I would ever so much like to see what other disguises you have."

I shake my head. "Not today.

Holmes huffs. "Are my services needed?"

"I don't think so." Reaching back into the console, I pull out a rawhide bone I decided to keep if I needed something to amuse Holmes. "Here, this should keep you busy while you wait."

Holmes refuses to take the bone. "You expect me to sit in the car for at least an hour? That's animal cruelty."

Fiona turns to face Holmes. "Try to be a good sport. We are only thinking about you. With the looks of Mr. Oppenheimer's security, he may have guard dogs on the property. It really is for your safety."

Silence.

"She's right, Holmes. It was a close call with the Doberman. What if I promise you a walk on the beach after we're done?"

Fiona shakes her head. "Derrick, don't you remember, we have one more suspect to visit today? By the time we are done it will be getting dark."

Holmes reluctantly takes the rawhide bone from my still outstretched hand and jumps down behind the seat. "Fine."

I drive up the impressively long driveway and park under a tree so that Holmes won't get overheated.

Fiona and I approach Mr. Oppenheimer's cherry red front door and are greeted by the man himself. He matches the photo Ms. Burke sent us perfectly with his white-grey hair, tanned face and designer grey suit. "Forbes surely has prompt employees."

Fiona gives me a quick glance. "Yes, we are."

"Perfect. Follow me."

Thankful for a stroke of luck, we follow Mr. Oppenheimer around the large Tudor inspired home to the back garden. It goes on for at least two acres and is filled with fountains and sculptured gardens straight out of Europe. "This is where I would like the interview to take place and where the photos should be taken."

Fiona nods. "The gardens rival several I've seen in Europe. It is a perfect place to talk of your success."

My partner is a natural at following a suspect's lead. Even I am starting to believe she works for *Forbes*.

Mr. Oppenheimer glances over at me. "Aren't you going to take some scouting photographs?"

I nod, pull out my phone, and walk around the first level of the garden taking pictures. The garden is green and vibrant as if it were in England getting constant rain. It really is a spectacular achievement knowing how dry it is most of the year in Southern California. When I get back to Fiona, I can see our time is up.

As Mr. Oppenheimer leads us back toward his impressive home, he turns to Fiona. "I am sorry I couldn't help you with your inquiry about the Health Nut. I never leave Bel Air. If I need anything in the city, I have my assistant fetch it for me."

Fiona truly is a master at what she does. She found a way to sneak in a question about the restaurant. "That is alright. I can find out where it is located with a simple Google search." Fiona shakes Mr. Oppenheimer's hand. "We appreciate your time."

Mr. Oppenheimer beams. "It was my pleasure. Please let me know when you have a confirmed date. Remember I have approval of the location and the clothing selection."

Fiona nods. "Yes, of course. Thank you again for the tour of your spectacular gardens."

He puffs out his chest with pride, then turns and struts toward his eleven-bedroom mansion. Fiona and I walk back to the car in silence. I open the door for her and then settle in behind the driver's seat even more confused than ever about Mr. Oppenheimer. "When I first saw Mr. Oppenheim, I was convinced he was the killer. He is so smooth and polished. And there is something sinister about how he acquired so much wealth. But having spoken with him, I'm not so certain."

Fiona buckles her seatbelt with a bit too much emphasis by slamming the belt into the clip lock. "We have been played. Ms. Burke put Oppenheim on the list to waste our time. I truly hate the competitive nature of detectives."

My gut tells me she is right. Oppenheim was never a suspect.

Holmes perks up in the back seat. "What did I miss?"

I turn on the engine and head back down the long

winding driveway. "I'll tell you later." Eyeing Fiona seething next to me, I can tell the last thing she wants to do is rehash the interview with Mr. Oppenheim.

Fiona scrolls through her messages and bursts out, "He has to be kidding. Today of all days."

"What's wrong?"

She throws her hair back off her shoulders. "It appears absence does not make the heart grow fonder. I've been dumped, by text no less."

My blood burns. The guy seemed like a jerk for ignoring her texts but the least he could do is dump her in person. "The guy is a total coward."

Fiona fights back tears. "He knows if he tried to do it in person, I'd punch his face in." She forms two fists. "Then I'd use my Thai boxing skills to break an arm and a leg."

Holmes pops his head up once we are clear of the gate cameras. "He would deserve that and more. You are well rid of him."

I know from the two times I've been dumped you never feel grateful. It hurts. "I've been there myself. The best thing to do is bury yourself in work."

She nods. "Brilliant idea." She pulls her phone out of her bag. "Ms. Burke doesn't say if our last suspect is home or not, but I say let's go to his place and maybe we will get lucky and surprise him."

I reach over and pat her hand. "Now, that's the spirit." But I know deep down she is still feeling the pain of being rejected. A pain that lingers far longer than it should. "So where to?"

"Mr. Carter lives in what I think you call the valley. The address is two thousand eleven Long Valley Road."

"Interesting. That is in Hidden Hills, a very exclusive part of the valley. Seems Mr. Carter is doing quite well for himself."

She turns to me still a bit ticked off. "Are all wizards a bunch of puffed-up blowhards?"

I point out the obvious. "You've seen my bungalow."

She turns away from me. "Point taken."

Holmes remains oblivious to the tension in the car, he's too busy looking out the window as we head back down into the heart of Los Angeles. "How far away is Hidden Hills? I would really like to stretch my legs."

"It's at least a forty-minute drive. There's a local park not far from here I'll take you for a quick walk, okay?"

Holmes mutters under his breath. "If that is the best you can do."

Fifteen minutes later, Holmes and I are strolling along a path that winds between a few scattered mature trees and a large expanse of lawn. Holmes turns up his nose as we pass a Labradoodle doing its business on the lawn. The owner, a middle-aged blond in a yoga outfit, dutifully bends down and picks it up with a park-supplied doggie bag. I must admit I am grateful to Mr. Bullock for creating Holmes with no need of bodily functions. He can enjoy a treat every once and a while and nothing happens. The food must be reabsorbed into his body somehow. I wish I had such a skill. Bathroom visits waste so much time. But wizards can't alter their bodies or its function, so I'm out of luck.

I let Holmes back into the car and find Fiona with her head turned, trying to hide the fact she has been crying. Part of me wants to give her a giant hug and tell her she is well rid of the jerk, but she is my work partner, so I pretend I didn't see anything. I start up the car and head back onto the 405 freeway. "Why don't you guys relax? By the looks of the traffic, it may take more than forty minutes to get to the valley."

Holmes sits looking out the side window as usual while Fiona stares straight ahead. Then she leans her seat back and closes her eyes. "I didn't sleep well last night. I'll just rest for a moment."

In less than five minutes she is sound asleep. With her head slumped to the side and her hair forming a giant curtain over her face, she looks so fragile. While my partner and sidekick take a nap, I weave in and out of traffic like the veteran Zoomer driver I am. Making my way onto the freeway, I drive further and further away from the hustle and bustle of the main part of the valley and out toward the open spaces of Hidden Hills. It's a place where there is enough room to have horses, goats, and a small army of lamas. It is a nice visual break from the heart of the city.

Holmes suddenly pops up in the back seat. In seconds his nose is pressed to the window taking in the changing view. "Look, wide open spaces. "

I crack his window just a bit so he can enjoy the scent of meadow grass and clean air. "Breath deep."

He does just that as I turn left onto Hidden Valley

Road, I take in the mix of Spanish style mansions and ranch houses. I stop two doors down from the unassuming white stucco ranch house where wizard suspect number three resides.

Fiona's eyes pop open when she hears me shut off the engine. "We are here already?"

I laugh. "It actually took almost an hour to get here."

She gazes out at the ranch house of our suspect. "I was expecting a real ranch. This is just a large white house with an expanse of green lawn in the front."

Holmes grumbles as he moves to the other side of the car. "I don't think you can have one of those in the city."

Fiona's gaze follows Holmes. "Oh, my. That is a strange looking animal. What is it?"

I lean over her and smile. "It's an alpaca. They are distantly related to camels. Isn't it cute? I love the tousled hair on their heads. But don't get too close, they spit."

Fiona moves her seat up to get a better look at the same time forcing me to lean back. "Where are they from?"

"South America. Having alpacas and llamas has become quite trendy with the wealthy. They are far more exotic than a horse and easier to care for."

Fiona's gaze shifts back to the suspect's white ranch house. "But the home is unassuming. It can't possibly cost as much as Oppenheimer's fancy mansion."

I give her a knowing smile. "That simple ranch

house is probably worth over six million dollars. It has to be on at least two acres."

Fiona shakes her head in disbelief. "California real estate is crazier than the London market."

"I think you are just stalling. Aren't you ready to cold call Mr. Carter?"

She reaches into her purse and pulls out a makeup bag. She unzips it and checks herself in the visor mirror. Letting out a sigh, she puts on a new coat of lipstick and powders her face. Giving me her best smile, she says, "Now I am."

I open the door for her and whisper in her ear. "At least there is no security surveillance like at Mr. Oppenheimer's."

"Let's hope we don't get a door slammed in our face."

I cross my fingers behind my back and wish for a bit of luck. So far, our investigation into Peter Hamlyn's death has gone nowhere. Mr. Bullock will not be pleased by our lack of progress. We walk up the concrete and brick path to a large wooden double door that has the perfect rustic ranch feel. Fiona places her French manicured finger on the doorbell, which thankfully is an old, fashioned one not one with a camera built in.

We stand for a good minute waiting for someone to arrive. Just as Fiona is ready to turn on her bootie heels, a tall lanky man approaches the door dressed all in tweed as if he is ready to go hunting fox in England. He opens the door with not a hint of fear or apprehension in his eyes. "Welcome. I had a feeling someone from

WI-6 would arrive at my door. It appears I was correct."

His perfect British Eton school accent fits his outfit to a tee.

Fiona strolls into the main room as if she owns the house. It has high peaked ceilings accented with wood beams. A two-story stone fireplace takes center stage. She sits down on one of the comfortable looking brown leather club chairs. "You are correct, Mr. Carter. We are here because of your affiliation to the late Mr. Hamlyn."

Mr. Carter motions for me to sit in the other club chair while he sits down in the middle of a large white sofa. "It is true. I knew Mr. Hamlyn. We went to Wizarding School together. We also had a similar passion for healthy eating."

Fiona looks over at a clear teacup sitting on the side table next to the sofa. "What is that delectable aroma?"

Mr. Carter gives her a lopsided grin. "Sakura tea. It is made from cherry blossoms and is a wonderful antioxidant. Peter...Mr. Hamlyn served it in his restaurant at my suggestion. Would you like to try some?"

Fiona nods. "If it tastes as good as its fragrance."

The idea of a tea made from cherry blossoms has no appeal for me. Mr. Carter seems too upper crust and pulled together to be a killer. Yet to make sure, I cast a character detection spell to be sure. My spell finds no danger thankfully. While Mr. Carter disappears to get Fiona her tea, I gaze around the austere living room. It has two pieces of monotone abstract artwork and a large live tree in the corner and that is it.

Mr. Carter returns with another clear teacup with a pink flower floating in the middle. It does have a pleasant fragrance as he wizzes by me and hands the cup to Fiona. She takes a sip, closing her eyes to savor the flavor. "It is quite pleasant. Thank you."

He nods. "I was sorry to hear of Mr. Hamlyn's death. We had lost touch over the last two years. Yet, I am sad he is no longer with us. He was a vibrant person taken too soon."

Normally I would think his response is canned, but there is an unmistakable sincerity in his voice. "I wish I could help your investigation...I truly do."

I stand up knowing we are getting nowhere. "I'm sure you have other things to do. I appreciate you taking the time to speak with us."

Fiona takes a long sip from her teacup reluctant to part with it. "Thank you for introducing me to Sakura tea, Mr. Carter."

"It was my pleasure. Best of luck to you." He gives Fiona a slight bow and then closes the door.

I let out a deep sigh as we walk back to the car, empty handed once again. "We need all the luck we can get. Are most cases this hard to solve?"

It's Fiona's turn to sigh. "They can be. I admit I was hoping this one would be solved quickly so I had some time to sightsee. At this rate, that is not going to be possible."

She's right. After the long drive out to Hidden Hills, the short interview felt hardly worth it. I help Fiona back into the car. "Well, there is no doubt Mr. Carter gave us nothing."

I walk over to the driver side, kick the tire, and get behind the wheel.

Holmes turns his gaze away from the alpaca and nudges my shoulder. "Why the glum face?"

"Mr. Bullock is going to be less than thrilled by our lousy report."

Holmes still hovers over my shoulder. "Maybe there is something you're missing. What does your gut tell you?"

Mr. Bullock's words repeated from his creation. "My gut thinks he is not the guy, and neither is Mr. Oppenheim."

Fiona nods. "I have no idea why Ms. Burke put him on the killer list."

I let out a sigh. "I drove a long way to find he is not our guy. Worst of all we need to start a whole new killer list."

"Well, at least it wasn't a wasted trip. Fiona now knows what an alpaca looks like."

She chuckles. "That is true." Then she sucks back a breath and soon is gasping for air.

I grab her hand. "What's wrong Fiona?"

"Mr. Carter...the Sakura tea he gave me..." She takes a gulp of air. "It was..." then she lets out a last gasp. "Poisoned."

11

NOW WHAT?

My wizarding instincts kick in as I stare at Fiona's face growing paler by the moment. Closing my eyes, I harken back to what I'd seen Mr. Kumar do in similar situations and cast a time freeze spell. I'm breaking a major rule of the Twelfth Order, but hopefully the Exemplary Wizard will understand that I had no choice but to use their powerful magic to save my partner's life.

Holmes hovers next to me just as concerned about Fiona. "Is she going to be alright? Can't you cast a spell to heal her?"

I shake my head. "If she were human, I could...but she is a shifter. I don't have a specific spell for that. I put her in time-stasis until I can get her some help."

As if I'm on autopilot, I race back to WI-6 head-quarters taking all the short cuts I've memorized from my years of Zoomer driving. I send a frantic text to Mr.

Bullock and hope he has a doctor that can help her. A pit balls up in my stomach from using forbidden magic. I can only hope there are no repercussions with the Twelfth Order.

As I pull into the parking structure at headquarters, I glance over at Fiona's face that is as pale as a sheet. At least her close call with death will have been worth it. This treacherous move by Mr. Carter proves his guilt.

Holmes races beside me as I throw open the car door and sweep Fiona into my arms. I race to the elevator and snap my finger to open the door. Fiona's head lies limp on my arm as Holmes stands and pushes the button to Mr. Bullock's floor.

"She is a fighter. I sense she will survive."

I want to believe him knowing full well dogs can smell cancer and death. "I hope you are right. Anyone looking at her now would think she is dead already."

Holmes stands firm in his belief. "It is true her skin color is alarmingly pale. But I smell no hint of death."

I'm glad Fiona is unconscious and can't hear our conversation.

The door pops open and a friendly face greets us. Scott races to my side to help me carry Fiona. "What happened to your partner?"

"I think she was poisoned by one of the suspects."

"Your text was rather cryptic, but we have a doctor as you requested."

Mr. Bullock himself reaches over and takes Fiona from my arms. A bed materializes in front of him. Placing her gently on the bed, he puts his hand on her forehead, looks up at me and then back at her. "I will tell no one what you did to save her."

I shouldn't be surprised he can sense my use of Order magic, but I am. I don't know if I believe him about not telling the Exemplary Wizard, but it is a risk I had to take. "Sir, my stasis spell will be wearing off soon. Is there a doctor who can help her nearby?"

"Yes, he should be here any moment." Mr. Bullock points to a chair. "Rest."

As much as I want to stay near Fiona, I do what he says. Carrying Fiona for such a long distance has worn me out. Not to mention she weighs far more than I thought.

A white-haired older man dressed in white scrubs strides through the door carrying a small black leather bag. He places it next to Fiona, who remains motionless on the bed Mr. Bullock conjured. I look into the doctor's dark brown eyes. "Please save her."

As he opens the bag, I can see there are no standard doctor instruments inside like a stethoscope. Instead, he holds out a device the size of a small calculator. He uses it to scan Fiona's body from head to toe. "First let me say whatever magic you used surely helped save Ms. Singh's life. It appears it froze the anaphylactic shock she was experiencing, which would have been life threatening if not fatal. Let's find out what triggered it."

I lean closer thrilled at the news that Fiona is not going to die. "Is it like what happened with Mr. Hamlyn? Does she have a toxic level of vitamin A in her system?"

The doctor takes a hold of her index finger and gives it a prick. "We are about to find out." He places a drop of blood on a small square device and within a minute it flashes purple. Wizard gadgets always remind me of the ones in James Bond movies, only ours are real.

The doctor's brow furrows as he looks at the results. "What did Ms. Singh eat or drink before this happened."

"She had a cup of Sakura tea. Was it spiked?"

The doctor taps something into his device. "Now the results make sense. It seems Ms. Singh had a severe allergic reaction to consuming cherry blossoms."

He pulls a syringe out of his bag and injects something into Fiona's arm. "She should come around shortly."

First, I'm reeling from the news Fiona truly will be all right, then from the fact that Mr. Carter appears to be innocent. I should be excited, but instead I dread trying to come up with a new killer list when the prospects are running slim.

I stroke Fiona's hand as her eyes flutter open. She struggles to sit up but is unsuccessful. "Mr. Carter tried to kill me!"

I smooth her long hair out of her face. "No. You had an allergic reaction."

Her brow creases and she looks up at me with total confusion. "He's not the killer?"

I squeeze her hand tight. "No. You had an allergic reaction to the cherry blossom tea."

She parses her lips. "I guess that makes sense. I do have hay fever."

Feeling a bit self-conscious knowing Mr. Bullock is watching me, I gently let go of her hand. "I'm sorry, but it looks like we need to draw up a new killer list."

Mr. Bullock nods. "I told Ms. Burke to give you two a hand with the killer list but it has not worked out as I hoped."

A pang of recognition hits me. Ms. Burke might be sabotaging us on purpose. Maybe the boys of *The Pit* put her up to it. Regardless, we need to go back to doing our own legwork. "I'm sure she was only trying her best to help. Sometimes leads don't pan out."

Mr. Bullock gives me a half smile. "Said like you are someone that has been a detective far longer than four days."

Has it only been that long? Things have been so action packed since I took the job at WI-6, it feels like it's been at least a month. "I had no idea how hard detective work is. I have the utmost respect for my colleagues."

He has no reaction at first and then nods. I hope he realized I meant it sincerely.

Mr. Bullock bends down next to Fiona. "I want you to take tomorrow off." He glances over at Holmes and me. "I think the boys need some time to pull together a new list anyway."

Somehow, he's managed to make me go from feeling proud of what I've done in four days to a complete failure. "Yes, you need your rest. It's been quite a day."

Fiona wrestles herself out of the conjured bed and stands defiantly next to the doctor and Mr. Bullock. "I will be right as rain in a few hours."

The doctor shakes his head. "Ms. Singh, I don't think you have any idea how close to death you were today. If it wasn't for your partner's quick actions, things might have ended quite differently."

Fiona looks over at me with a look of appreciation and then pain. Could she know what a risk I took using magic of the Order to save her life?

Holmes sits next to her feet. "You had me quite worried. I am so glad you are going to recover."

She bends down to pat him on the head and loses her balance. I race to her side to keep her from toppling off the bed. "I know how much you don't want to let us down, but you really do need to get some rest. I'll take you back to the hotel."

Mr. Bullock shakes his head. "That won't be necessary. My assistant will take her home. You need to get to *The Pit* and come up with your next course of action." Then he looks down at a text on his phone and vanishes into thin air.

MS. BURKE HOVERS OVER ME AS I SIT IN THE DARK depths of *The Pit*. "I'm sorry the last leads didn't pan out. It's because..." She looks over at Smith and Ross. "You know, peer pressure."

I don't care what she says. It's obvious I can't trust her. "No problem. Sure, you were doing your best."

Holmes nudges my hand that is resting on my desk. "She isn't being on the up and up."

I do the cut sign on my neck hoping he understands it is not safe to speak freely in *The Pit*.

At first, he has a confused look then a spark of recognition hits his eyes. "Do you think we should look at the restaurant footage one more time?"

The question proves he understood me. Ms. Burke took it upon herself to watch the last half of the footage for us. Now I know Fiona and I need to review the security footage ourselves. "We need to head out. I just thought of a lead."

Holmes nods but as soon as we hit the door, Ross blocks our path. I may be as tall as he is, but he's double my weight.

He grins, knowing his obvious advantage over me. "I was told to make sure you do your investigative work in house."

The smug tone in his voice is hiding the fact that he is lying.

Holmes growls and moves close enough to bite Ross in the leg. Thankfully Ross's bull mastiff is sound asleep and snoring next to his desk.

A flash of red hair and Ms. Burke is by my side. She smiles up at Ross. "I think we can make an exception for today. Mr. Dunne did almost lose his partner."

Ross glares at Ms. Burke, then reluctantly steps aside. As I push past him, he says in my ear. "You're on my shit list, Dunne."

Fantastic, I think as Holmes, and I pile into the elevator.

Holmes senses my dismay. "I don't know exactly what is going on but the tone in *The Pit* has gone from unaccepting and annoyed with you to outright hostility."

I sigh as we exit the elevator and head towards the car. "It's been a day."

Someone grabs my arm and pulls me down next to a large black Escalade. "We need to talk."

I stare into the eyes of Scott. "I'm getting the distinct impression I'm not wanted at WI-6. Are you here to give me a heads up?"

Scott's gaze shifts to Holmes. "Of a sort. We can't talk here." He hands me one of his business cards with an address written on the back. "Be at this location at nine o'clock."

I suddenly feel like I've slipped into a Sherlock Holmes caper. "All right."

Scott eyes Holmes once again. "Come alone."

I STAND IN FRONT OF THE IMPRESSIVE ART DECO edifice of the Pier Hotel in downtown LA wondering if I'm walking into a trap. Scott has always been totally in my corner, but things seem to have taken a turn to the dark side at WI-6. The fact that he specifically asked for Holmes not to come with me has my hackles up. Yet, if I want answers, I know I must take a chance. The shiny brass door to the hotel leads into a classic black marble floor entry surrounded by a sea of white walls. Two large deco chandeliers illuminate the lobby. I smile noticing not one pot light in sight.

The hotel has an old school Hollywood glamor I'm glad wasn't destroyed when they renovated the place. I stride over to the etched glass elevator doors and push the brass button to the sixth floor. The hotel is quiet except for several guests sitting together in the plush dark blue velvet club chairs that inhabit a small room next to the elevators. The door glides open, and I smile as an attractive blond steps out dressed in a tight black cocktail dress and killer heels. She waves when she sees her friends seated in the chairs.

When the door opens on the sixth floor Scott greets me. "Derrick, I'm so glad you're here. I thought there was a good chance you wouldn't come."

I shrug my shoulders. "I've been known to be way too curious for my own good."

Scott moves quickly down the hallway, slides a keycard into room 607, and pulls me inside. "Sorry, I'm a bit paranoid." He motions to a blue velvet sofa in what is a surprisingly luxurious suite. "Sit. I need to talk fast. Mr. Bullock is expecting me back at the office in forty minutes."

I sink down into the cushion still feeling leery. "So, Mr. Bullock doesn't know you are talking to me."

He plops down on a matching club chair. "No. He wouldn't approve. He likes his detectives to figure things out on their own. But after what happened to your partner today, I've decided it's only fair you should know what's going on."

My shoulders relax a bit. My gut was right. Something is off at WI-6. "Okay. This is obviously more than a newbie getting hazed by his colleagues."

Scott smiles. "Yes, that is happening as well. Ross and Smith are famous for their schoolboy ways." Scott eyes the impressive view of the Los Angeles skyline out the window. "But there is something more going on."

Scott reminds me of the Exemplary Wizard and his love for dragging out important news. "Let me guess. The killer list Ms. Burke created was totally to throw us off track."

Scott lets out a quick breath. "Yes, I'm glad you figured it out. But you don't know who instigated it. It wasn't your fellow detectives, it was their boss."

At first, I'm confused. Mr. Bullock is everyone's boss. Then it hits me. "You mean Mr. Pierre. But why? I thought he liked me."

Scott shakes his head. "It has nothing to do with you personally. It has everything to do with Mr. Pierre's vendetta against Mr. Bullock. You see, he wants my boss's job. He has for the last couple of years. He was passed over when they hired my boss." He gives me a knowing smile. "And you should know I'm not Mr. Bullock's personal assistant. That's a cover. I'm his spy."

The plot thickens just like in the movies. Here I thought I was walking into a normal work situation. It turns out I've walked into a feud to rival Thor and Loki's. "I wish you had given me a heads up a bit earlier."

He hangs his head. "It's been almost impossible to

get away. Mr. Bullock obviously wants me to stay on top of what Mr. Pierre is up to. But tonight, thankfully he is out celebrating his victory. He thinks you are going to quit which will humiliate Mr. Bullock as he handpicked you. The board of WI-6 were not pleased as they had their own candidate. Not to mention the fact that they are not fans of the Twelfth Order."

A smile crosses my face at the thought that little old me is in the crosshairs of a show down at WI-6. "Turns out I've been given a pretty important role without even knowing it."

Scott stands up. "You have. And I need you to not only find Mr. Hamlin's killer, I need you to help me foil Mr. Pierre's plan."

My shoulders suddenly feel the weight of his words. "I'll do my best." I stand up and touch Scott's shoulder. "Thank you for risking your life to warn me."

He reaches out to grab the door and then stops. "Let's hope together we can foil the plot and still be left standing."

TAPPING THE WINDOW OF MY BMW, HOLMES'S HEAD pops up. "You have a good nap? How about a walk by the beach like you wanted?"

He sits up in the back seat. "You look a bit pale. Was your meeting satisfactory?"

I hate lying to him, but Scott had to have a reason for not wanting me to bring Holmes to the meeting.

"Not really. Another waste of time. It's been an exhausting day full of close calls and disappointment."

He nods. "Sounds like you need the walk on the beach more than I do. But it's dark."

I get behind the wheel and start the engine. "I know the perfect place that lights up the sand for miles, the pier."

Holmes sits up and barks his approval. "Brilliant. Make haste!"

I laugh as I pull out of the hotel parking structure and head toward the freeway. Navigating the on ramp, I zig zag through traffic until I hit the carpool lane. I conjure a likeness of Krissy to fool the highway patrol.

Holmes snickers. "You use magic in the most amusing ways."

"Why not conjure a beautiful girl by my side." A pang of loss hits me. If only I had Fiona next to me. I tap the screen and dial her number at the hotel. A faint sound comes through the speakers. "Who is it? I asked not to be disturbed."

"It's Derrick. Sorry, I used a bit of magic to reach you. I wanted to make sure you were feeling better."

Her voice brightens. "My wizard in shining armor. Thank you for rescuing me."

There is a childlike quality in her voice. It must be the drugs they gave her. "It was my pleasure. Are you feeling better?"

"Yes, a bit woozy still but I will be at work tomorrow. I just need a good night's sleep."

I wish she wasn't so dedicated to her work. "I'm

sure Mr. Bullock would be more than happy to give you a day off to recover."

The sound of a glass clinking comes through the speaker. "I will be fine. I'm just having a spot of oolong and then I'll go back to sleep."

It's amazing how the British can drink tea all day and still sleep like babies. "Good night, partner."

She clicks off and Holmes nudges my shoulder. "You care for her, admit it."

"What are you? My matchmaker too?"

He barks enthusiastically. "What is wrong with wanting to see two nice people together? She's free now. Plus, you saved her life. That has to win you some points."

I chuckle. "You are right about that. I'm not looking for anyone."

Holmes sits back in his seat. "I think you have grieved long enough."

Not something I haven't heard from many of my friends. "As fantastic as Fiona is, I'm not ready yet."

We hit the Santa Monica Pier in record time thanks to my little dummy trick. I let Holmes out of the car and his nose sniffs the air as he pulls on his leash. I don't blame him for wanting to get out in the fresh air when he has been cooped up in the car most of the day. I let him dictate the pace as he pulls me along the edge of the pier and close to the water's edge. I breathe in the salty ocean air hoping it can clear my mind as well as my lungs. Instead of improving my mood, a sharp pang in my right temple signals I have a headache coming on. I stop in the slick sand and yank on Holmes' lead. "I need a break for a moment."

He sits down looking out at the ocean while I rub my temples in hopes of chasing the headache away.

"It's understandable that your head would hurt after the day you've had."

The unmistakable British voice of Mr. Kumar. A voice that could only mean one thing—I'm in trouble. "Sir, I was going to contact you as soon as I got home. You know I would have never broken my oath unless it was a true emergency. A matter of life and death."

"Don't worry, the Exemplary Wizard doesn't know about your indiscretion. I know I would have done the same thing myself. Ms. Singh is a talented woman who is way too young to die."

I let out a deep sigh that Holmes doesn't notice. He's too busy enjoying the fresh air and watching the sea gulls scurry after sand crabs.

"I'm glad you understand. May I ask why you reached out?"

"Derrick, even though you are no longer officially part of the Order I am still watching over your safety. As you found out tonight there is great turmoil at WI-6. Had I known, I would have never let you take the job. But having you in WI-6 will help the Order as well. Mr. Bullock is an ally, Mr. Pierre is not. He must not succeed with his takeover plan."

Fantastic. I've been thrust into a rival wizard division feud. "Sir, what can I do to foil Mr. Pierre?"

"You must find the killer and embarrass him. That will put him back in his place."

I let out a nervous chuckle. "That's all."

Holmes looks up at me. "Is everything all right?"

Anything but, I think to myself, but I answer, "I'm just tired. Let's head back to the car."

Holmes reluctantly turns towards the pier as I go back to my conversation with Mr. Kumar. "Do you know who killed Mr. Hamlyn?"

"No, but I know how he was killed. Someone spiked his carrot smoothie everyday with extra vitamin A. Find the person who had access to his smoothies, and you have your killer."

My mind reels. "You mean he really was killed by carrots? I thought it was just a joke."

"Not at all. The amount of vitamin A found in carrots can indeed be fatal. Over time, heavy consumption builds up in the bloodstream. In Mr. Hamlyn's case, because of his passion for juicing, as few as twenty-four carrots could have pushed him over the edge."

As Mr. Kumar exits my mind, the lights of the Santa Monica pier bounce off the sand blinding me. I try to process Mr. Kumar's words. The killer is the person who had access to Peter's smoothies. The one person who would have had it daily is his boyfriend. Why would he want the love of his life dead? "No, it can't be him."

Holmes looks up at me and barks. A reminder that the people whizzing around me are going to think I'm crazy if I keep talking out loud. I pat him on the head. "Good boy. Let's head back home."

We walk at a brisk pace back to my car. It only

takes a few minutes to pull up to my Craftsman bungalow.

As soon as I open the door, Holmes pins me to the entry wall. "You better tell me what is going on. I've never seen you talk to yourself before. Is this case getting to you?"

The sound of concern in his voice seems real. Yet, I still have Scott's words lingering in the back of my mind—*come alone*. With Fiona out of the picture, he had to mean Holmes.

I pat him on the head. Thanks for your concern." My stomach growls, reminding me that unlike Holmes, I need food to survive. "I think I've waited way too long to eat. That explains the headache and my growling stomach."

Holmes nods and nudges me toward the refrigerator. "Then either conjure something or raid the fridge."

Interesting how he is picking up more and more American words. "I'm too tired to use magic." Pulling open the freezer, I'm faced with mostly empty shelves. I realize I either need to go shopping or conjure up a week's worth of groceries. The only food on the shelves are a half-eaten gallon of cookie dough ice cream and a frozen dinner so covered in ice I can't tell what it is. Curious, I pull out the carton and run water over it. I hold up the soaked carton. "Look, it's a tikka masala dinner! The perfect tribute to Fiona."

Holmes snickers. "I doubt she would consider it real food from her country."

I toss the plastic container in the microwave. "My stomach doesn't care."

Holmes joins me by the tiny dinner table. "It doesn't smell half bad. Although I doubt the small portion will give you much sustenance."

I love it when he uses big words. The tikka masala vanishes in four big bites. I top it off with the rest of the cookie dough ice cream. Rubbing my slightly bulging belly I say, "I'm stuffed. Now I have the energy to solve the case. Let's watch those tapes."

Tossing the plastic dinner container in the trash, I pull open my laptop and start scrolling through the security videos.

Holmes rests his head on the table. "You need a second set of eyes. I may not see color as well as you, but as far as motion and detail goes, my vision is superior."

For once I'm not irritated by his snotty tone. Without my partner, I need my sidekick's help. Scrolling through a month's worth of footage we both see nothing out of the ordinary. Just customers going inside the restaurant eating and then leaving and a few food deliveries. Peter Hamlyn arriving every morning, sometimes with his boyfriend, sometimes not. Not once do I see anyone making a smoothie in the kitchen. The only smoothie making is happening at the juice bar by either Peter or one of the girls that work at the restaurant. I continue scrolling through the footage even though it is getting hard to keep my eyes open. The events of today have finally caught up with me.

I'm about to close the laptop when Holmes thrusts his paw across the keyboard to stop me. "Go back to the part where Peter is walking toward the juice bar."

I scroll back and then move slowly forward again. At first, I can't see anything unusual, then I notice a flash of motion behind Peter.

Holmes nudges the screen. "Slow the tape down further. I think you might have found your killer."

I do what he says, and the blur becomes visible. It's a person—an everyman—it's Detective Smith.

12
____

WHO DONE IT?

Walking into *The Pit*, I've never been filled with as much tension as this morning. How am I going to confront Detective Smith? I let out an internal sigh of relief when I see he is noticeably absent. In fact, Ross and the other detectives are gone too. The only other detective I see this morning is my partner. I walk over to her and try not to show concern in my eyes. Fiona still is frightfully pale. "Good to see you back at work."

She gives me a weak smile. "There is too much going on to stay home any longer."

Little does she know how much more is on our plate since yesterday? "Right. Did you see the text to report to Mr. Pierre?" I wish I could warn her that he is enemy number one, but *The Pit* has more cameras and microphones than the Washington DC CIA office.

She shrugs and looks back into the deepest part of *The Pit*. "He isn't here yet."

Perfect, I have a chance to warn her. "I feel the need to go to the bathroom. What about you?"

Thankful she understands my meaning, she starts walking toward the door. "Yes. I do too." She gives me a wink, a hint of the old Fiona returning. "Guess we both had too much coffee this morning."

We stroll out the door and down the hallway to the bathroom. I cast a privacy spell on the restroom and join her inside. "I don't totally trust my spell, so I'll be a bit cryptic. Things have been flipped on their ear since yesterday. Don't let anyone in *The Pit,* including Mr. Pierre get you alone."

Her brow furrows hearing the concern in my voice. "Is it that dire?"

I sigh. "Worse."

Hearing a noise in the hallway, I hold my breath as Ms. Burke comes striding through the door. Sensing we are about to get in trouble, Fiona bends over and begins making retching noises.

Ms. Burke stands with her hands thrust on her hips. "What are you doing in the restroom with your partner Mr. Dunne?"

I race to Fiona's side. "My partner is still not feeling well. She asked me to come with her in case she passes out."

Ms. Burke's eyes home in on my trouser zipper that is firmly shut. Satisfied we weren't trying to cover up a sexual liaison, she relaxes a bit and gently touches Fiona on the shoulder. "Should you be back at work? Maybe you need some more rest."

Fiona brushes her hair off her face and straightens

up. "No, I'm alright. My medication is beginning to kick in."

My partner is an expert liar. Something a good detective must easily master when they are being lied to all the time.

I give Ms. Burke a slight bow. "Ladies, as I am no longer needed, I will bid you good morning." I hear a chuckle as I exit the restroom.

Holmes sits with his head cocked to the side as I meander back to my desk. "What exactly is going on?"

I pat him on the head. "Don't worry, I didn't violate any rules."

A French accented voice sounds from behind me. "That is good to hear. I want you and your partner to meet me at my desk in five minutes."

I let out a sigh of relief he didn't hear more. "Certainly, sir. I was just about to finish up my report."

He says nothing as he turns his back to me and disappears into the darkness. Now I understand why he always treated me like a disease that infested his beloved *Pit*. I'm literally standing between the power he desperately wants and handing over another victory to his enemy. The tension I felt when I first arrived makes sense now. The bigger problem is not letting my knowledge affect my interactions with him. My new spy role for the Twelfth Order can never get off the ground if he senses something is off about me. Hopefully warning Fiona hasn't blown my cover either. Flashing on every James Bond movie I've ever seen, I have a newfound respect for the tightrope his character walks in every movie.

Fiona types up a report and hits send. She gives me a wink as we walk over to Mr. Pierre's desk. He looks up at us and twists his little mustache and smiles. "I see you are having no luck solving Mr. Hamlyn's murder."

I'm surprised he is so freely showing his glee. "Despite what our reports say, we are getting very close."

His gaze shifts to Fiona. "Ms. Singh, I would like you to join me for lunch."

She doesn't miss a beat. "Oh, sir, I am terribly sorry, but we have an appointment to interview a new suspect. In fact, we need to leave immediately."

Before he has a chance to say a thing, she speed walks toward the door. Once we get outside, I pull her next to me. "That was a fast move."

She walks briskly toward the elevator and pushes the button for the parking garage. "Sorry, hopefully I didn't blow our cover."

I step into the elevator and stay quiet wondering if Fiona might have made things worse.

The door slides open, and Fiona lets out a sigh of relief. "I'm so glad you warned me about Mr. Pierre. I would have gladly accepted the invitation to lunch. Who knows what would have happened to me?"

"Nothing good. We need to go someplace where I can fill you in on the rest."

She grabs my arm. "Has that much happened in just twelve hours?"

"You have no idea." I stop dead in my tracks when I spy detective Smith getting out of a black Pontiac sedan—alone. No Ross, no dog sidekick. I let go of

Fiona's arm. "You are about to find out another piece of the puzzle."

She follows my gaze. "I had a feeling Smith is involved somehow."

"And you'd be right. Just how much we are about to find out."

I race to block Mr. Smith's path as he moves quickly toward the elevator. "Just the man I want to speak with."

His ordinary face stares back at me with a well-practiced blank expression. "I'm busy."

"Oh, you've been busy alright." I signal Holmes and Fiona. "Follow me to my car. We need to talk."

He eyes a plan of escape toward the next level of the parking garage but Holmes grabs onto his left ankle and bites down. I give Smith a satisfied grin as the reality of how much he is outnumbered hits him. "We just need a minute of your time."

Surprisingly he doesn't put up a fight. He dutifully follows us to the car. Smith's confidence tells me he has already sent out an SOS to his partner Ross. I smile, knowing if he did text Ross, he will never get it. When I first spotted Smith, I used a spell to disabled his phone as well as the parking structure surveillance. As I'm back working for the Order, I have no fear of repercussions for using their magic.

Opening the back door, I signal for Smith to get in. Holmes reluctantly let's go of Smith's ankle and jumps onto the back seat next to him. Fiona squeezes in on the other side of Smith forming a protective sandwich.

I plop down in the passenger seat and turn to face

my suspect. "Why were you at the Health Nut on the twenty-first of November?"

His eye's lock in on mine. "I wondered how long it would take you to find me in the footage."

"Answer the question."

His gaze stays fixed on me. "I was on a case."

"What did Peter Hamlyn have to do with your investigation?"

"That information is classified. All you need to know is it was under Mr. Pierre's orders." He glares at Fiona squished next to him. "Tell your lackey to back off."

Fiona elbows his ribs. "If you think we are going to let you go with that kind of answer, you're stupider than I thought."

With my magic handcuffs off, I get to work and enter his mind. "There is no hiding from me now." I cruise through his brain until I get my answer. "Ah, so Mr. Pierre didn't trust Peter's use of magic."

Smith slams back in his seat. "Reading my mind is forbidden. You've broken a major WI-6 code."

I'll give Mr. Smith his due, he has bigger balls than I thought. "And what did your investigation discover?"

"You should know the answer to that after reading my mind."

I dig into his memory a bit more. "I had no idea WI-6 also monitors the use of magic."

"Yes, we investigate wizards who abuse their magic and other wizard-related crimes. Mr. Hamlyn was care-less, but never committed a crime with his magic."

I must admit I'm disappointed in his answer. Part

of me really hoped Mr. Pierre was the killer. "Right." I motion Fiona to open the door. "Have a good day, Detective Smith."

He slams the door in Fiona's face and screams out. "Screw you."

Fiona moves over to the driver's seat. "I hope you know we will be fired for that stunt."

I grin. "No, we won't. As much as Mr. Pierre thinks he is running the show, the person that hired us is—Mr. Bullock. We answer to him."

"True enough." Fiona sits back in her seat. "So, fill me in on the rest."

I eye Holmes still not knowing if I can trust him. For insurance, I cast a mock conversation spell. While I'm dishing the dirt to Fiona, Holmes hears a totally benign conversation about Fiona's doctor visits and medications.

After I fill her in, she looks like I felt last night. "I'm gobsmacked. I thought Mr. Pierre was the killer. That means we need to interview Mr. Jones immediately. It wouldn't hurt to revisit the hostess and Mr. Carter." She shivers. "I still think he's involved somehow."

"Right. Who do you want to talk to first?"

She pulls out her phone. "Let me call Mr. Jones. I'll tell him we need a bit more information because we are getting close to tracking down Peter's killer."

My gut tells me Mr. Jones is innocent. "I think he should be last."

Fiona scrolls through her messages, looking for the

phone numbers. "Fine, I'll call Miss Lake and Mr. Carter. One of them has to be the killer."

I give her a thumbs up. "We might get lucky." It never occurred to me how much luck plays into detective work until now.

Holmes perks up in the back seat. "I wouldn't cast my hopes on the boyfriend."

Fiona turns around a bit surprised. "Why, Holmes?"

"It's not a crime of passion, it's money based," Holmes says with conviction.

I nod. "I agree. My gut thinks so too." I wave at Fiona's phone. "Don't bother with Mr. Jones. Let's give Miss Lake and Mr. Carter a call."

Fiona hesitates before she dials the first number. "I hope your gut is right." She pushes in a number and a young woman's voice comes on the line. "This is Miss Lake. I don't recognize the number. Hope this is about the hostess job at Drake's."

Fiona puts on her best snooty American businesswoman voice. "Why yes, this is Ms. Haze from HR. Can you meet me at The Grove?"

Amazing. Fiona has a totally convincing American accent.

Miss Lake hesitates a second. "Um, you don't want me to come to the restaurant?"

Fiona gives me a confident smile. "No, Because of an internal problem we are meeting people at an alternate location."

"Okay, sure. Where and what time?"

Fiona hesitates for a second. "In a half an hour at the Fountain Bar."

"See you then."

I give Fiona a light applause. "You were amazing. Your American accent was as good as an actor's. She totally believed you were from HR."

Fiona grins ear to ear. "Why, thank you, partner."

"I must admit the Fountain Bar is a creative choice. Although I'm surprised you know about it."

She laughs. "The concierge at the hotel recommended the bar."

A pang of jealousy hits me. It's a popular place to meet on dates. "I'm not surprised it is a great place to have a drink. Especially at night when the fountain is all lit up."

Fiona nods. "I picked it because Miss Lake is a total wild card. Interviewing her in a highly visible location felt right. Besides, we can grab a bite after."

My stomach churns in agreement. "Perfect. Their burgers are one of the best in town."

Using my Zoomer skills, we make it to the Westside just in time. I stop at the curb. "Don't you think Miss Lake will recognize you? Aren't you going to shift into someone else?"

"Right." She chuckles. "I forgot I don't need to hide my gift from you." She closes her eyes and in mere seconds my beautiful Indian partner turns into a stereotypical California bleach blonde except for the severe black pant suit she is wearing. Fiona opens her purse, takes out a hair band and pulls her newly blonde locks into a bun. "Do I look like I work in HR?"

I give her a thumbs up and Holmes barks his

approval. "You look perfect. Now get the information we need to lock down the killer."

She gives Holmes the okay sign and disappears into the crowd. I park the car and put my credit card in the meter.

Holmes nudges my shoulder. "Aren't you going to follow her?"

I shake my head. "There is no need to risk being recognized by Miss Lake. I'll just cast a fly-on-the-wall spell to hear what they are saying. Do you want to see the interview as well?"

Holmes barks, he's so excited. "Of course." I conjure a viewing screen and Holmes jumps into the passenger seat. "Having a wizard owner sure has its benefits."

The viewing screen flickers for a second and then we are right there with Fiona as she sits down in a primo spot by the fountain. Having been to the bar before, I know Fiona had to have slipped the hostess at least forty dollars.

Miss Lake arrives dressed like a consummate hostess in a black jersey shirt and short black skirt. She smiles when Fiona waves her down. Miss Lake sits across from Fiona and hands her a copy of her resume. "I'm perfect for the job."

Fiona takes the paper and pretends to scroll through it. "Impressive. I think you will fit right in at Drake's."

Miss Lake's smile turns to a scowl. "You're not from Drake's HR. You're that detective. I have no idea how you disguised yourself so well, but I'd recognize that voice anywhere. Your American accent is lousy."

Holmes looks at me indignantly. "What is she talking about? Her accent is quite good."

I sigh realizing the obvious. "Ms. Burke tipped her off. We've been played again."

Fiona tries to play dumb. In a perfect American accent, she says. "I have no idea what you are talking about."

Miss Lake looks around the other tables. "Where is your hot partner?"

I must admit I'm a bit flattered she remembers me.

Fiona takes things in stride. "He's not here. Let's stop playing games. I have one question to ask you. Who are you working for?"

She scoffs at the question. "Nobody. Why else would I have agreed to meet with you?"

"You aren't very smart, Miss Lake. You should have asked Mr. Russel for more money."

Her shoulders tighten at the mention of the lawyer's name. "Who?"

Fiona reaches across the table and grabs her hand. Miss Lake tries to push her chair away but then stops. "I'll answer whatever you want for a hundred grand."

"Now you're getting smart." Fiona smiles. "Deal."

"The lawyer paid me to put a special liquid in Peter's smoothies every day. I thought it was just something to make him sick—not kill him." She looks around. "The police aren't going to take me in, are they?"

"No. They want Mr. Russel."

Fiona opens her purse to write out a check but pulls out the hundred grand I conjured instead. What Miss Lake doesn't know is the money will disintegrate in ten minutes.

Miss Lake's eyes grow wide as Fiona counts out the bills like she carries several hundred grand every day. Without saying a word, Miss Lake stuffs the money in her little back purse, flies out of her chair, and races across the patio. She soon disappears behind the fountain.

Holmes taps at the viewing screen with his paw. "Nice work! Your magic was seamless conjuring the money."

I open the driver's side door. "Thanks. I'm going to join Fiona. Why don't you take a nap?"

"After all that excitement?"

I pat him on the muzzle. "Be good. I might be awhile." Speed walking across the plaza I soon join Fiona sitting by the fountain. "Nicely done."

She smiles. "I can say the same for conjuring the money. You used magic to listen in, didn't you?"

I nod. "Guilty as charged. Just as guilty as Mr. Carter." Miss Lake's confession put everything together for me. "Your allergy attack was planned."

Fiona's eyebrows raise. "Why do you say that?"

"Mr. Carter is a wizard. A simple spell can tell him all your vulnerabilities."

Fiona squeezes my hand. "Well, I figured out what plan two was on the lawyers note."

"I don't doubt it. You're a great detective. Don't keep me in suspense.

She beams. "Mr. Russel and Mr. Carter are the same person."

We say in unison, "They both have the same lopsided smile."

I beam, knowing she truly listened to me. "You remembered when I told you wizards can't conjure away their physical traits? Mr. Carter could disguise himself quite well, but not the strange overbite he was born with."

"Precisely." Fiona reaches over and touches my hand. "He was the lawyer all along."

I look down at the table disgusted that once again a wizard has gone rogue. "Poor Peter died because of greed."

Fiona nods as she waves the waiter over to our table. "It's one of the prime motives of criminals. Even for wizards it appears."

Not the impression I want her to have of my kind. I smile and take in her bleach blonde hair. "I wish you could change back. I miss my partner."

"I wish I could too." Fiona smiles and rubs her stomach. "But I'm starving."

"Me too." I pick up the menu. "I'm tempted to order two burgers."

Fiona laughs. "Why not get half the menu?"

As if on cue, a blonde waiter appears next to our table. His sun-kissed highlights hint he likes to surf in his free time. "What would you like?"

Fiona points to the menu. "I'll have a grilled chicken salad and he'll have two avocado bacon burg-ers." The waiter turns to leave, and she adds, "Oh, and a bottle of champagne." She looks at me with pure joy on her face. "The case is solved. We need to celebrate!"

I look into my partner's eyes with admiration. "We do!" I hold up my water glass. "To Peter Hamlyn, whose unfortunate death was caused by carrots. May he rest in peace knowing his murderer has been found and will get the punishment he deserves."

Fiona clicks my water glass. "To a wizard and a shifter. The best detective partnership since Sherlock and Watson."

13

SHERLOCK & WATSON

Being summoned to Mr. Bullock's office used to set my nerves on edge. This morning for the first time I don't feel nervous even though the entire *Pit* crew is in attendance as well. Except for Mr. Klein, who according to Ms. Burke, is working a case in New York. Hopefully I will see more of him in the future.

Fiona stands next to me beaming as she takes in the fact that Smith, Ross, and Ms. Burke look like they have literally been stepped on. Disheveled doesn't even begin to describe their appearance. It's as if they slept with their clothes on all night and just got out of bed.

Holmes sits at my feet soaking up the fact he was the only canine sidekick allowed to attend the meeting. He looks up at me with admiration in his dark brown eyes. I feel a bit guilty that I ever doubted his loyalty. He proved to everyone he could keep the identity of the killer a secret. Mr. Carter was apprehended by WI-6 security bright and early this morning while trying to board a private jet. With a satisfied grin, I picture him being dragged away to face a fate worse than death.

Scott gives me a thumbs up as if he knows exactly what I'm smiling about. I'm glad I made my one ally at WI-6 proud. The icing on the cake is the fact that I helped expose Mr. Pierre. He stands in front of Mr. Bullock's desk twirling his mustache with so much vigor it must be painful. All I can do is gloat.

With his typical flourish, Mr. Bullock materializes next to Fiona and me. He looks out at *The Pit* crew with the satisfied smile of a cat who has caught a particularly large mouse. "I've gathered you together this morning so that we can celebrate the wonderful work of Mr. Dunne and Ms. Singh. They solved a very difficult case in merely a week." His eyes narrow in on Smith, Ross, and Ms. Burke. "This despite the fact that their fellow detectives put endless roadblocks in their way." He glares at Mr. Pierre knowing full well who instigated the plan. Then his gaze shifts back to the culprits. "I will speak with each one of you after the meeting about what disciplinary action will be taken."

Ms. Burke lets out a tiny gasp, while Ross puffs out his chest like it could buffer him from punishment. Smith looks like Mr. Bullock just punched him in the gut. His cheeks have turned red, and he stands slightly hunched over. Seeing their reaction only makes my smile grow broader. Solving the case feels amazing, but watching Ross, Smith and Burke get their comeuppance fills me with joy. Rarely have I seen justice be so swift. It makes me admire Mr. Bullock even more.

Having given Mr. Pierre and his crew a major glare

down, Mr. Bullock continues his speech. "Mr. Dunne and Ms. Singh come stand on either side of me."

Walking up to him, I feel I've finally arrived. After all the reconnaissance work I did for the Twelfth Order, I never had this type of acknowledgement from the Exemplary Wizard. He always treated me like a two headed stepchild.

Mr. Bullock pats me on the back. "Mr. Dunne, congratulations on the excellent job you did solving your first case. We here at WI-6 are honored you have joined our team."

Ross makes a gagging noise, not caring if he gets in any more trouble. His partners in crime however remain silent. I might as well take this opportunity to rub my success in Mr. Pierre's and his crew's faces. "Thank you, sir. It has been an honor to be accepted so eagerly into the WI-6 fold. I look forward to solving many more cases." I can't resist the temptation to get back at Ross, Smith, and Burke. "Hopefully in the future I will receive the support of my peers."

Mr. Bullock ignores my dig and holds out his hand to Fiona. "Ms. Singh, thank you for coming all the way to America to help Mr. Dunne solve the case. I know you have been an integral part of his success."

She shakes his hand and then her eyes lock in on Mr. Pierre. "Why thank you, sir. I have to say I thought I would receive a warmer welcome from my colleagues in *The Pit*. But I didn't let their high school antics deter me from solving the case."

Mr. Bullock signals Scott, who strolls across the room carrying two small gold boxes. He hands them over to his boss who quickly gives them to us. "These small gifts are token of my appreciation."

We both stand holding the boxes, not knowing whether to open them or not. Scott leans over and whispers in my ear, "Open the box, it will drive Mr. Pierre crazy."

Knowing the ongoing rivalry between him and Mr. Pierre, the gift must be something that will infuriate him. I signal Fiona and we open our boxes together. Inside the box is a little gold star resting on a pedestal. It is about as tall as a coffee mug. Not ostentatious, but big enough to make a statement. "Why thank you, sir. I will place it on my desk and cherish it always."

Muttering fills the room signaling that no such honor has been bestowed on the detectives of *The Pit*.

Fiona holds hers up as well. She makes a point to aim the star like a gun right at Ms. Burke's face. "Sir, it is a privilege to receive such an honor. I'm certain my superiors in London will be pleased."

He nods. "Tell Mr. Campbell I appreciate his kindness in lending you to our division."

My joy is short-lived when I realize what Mr. Bullock is saying. He knows the unusual American and UK murders aren't linked. There is no reason for Fiona to stay.

THE CIRCULAR DRIVE OF THE DEL MAR HOTEL IS particularly busy this afternoon. The fountain happily gurgles away ignoring the fact that I'm picking up

Fiona with a heavy heart. Having worked alone for years, I never knew how wonderful it could be to have a partner. The spark I felt when we first met, and again at our celebratory dinner last night, is still lying under the surface. But now I won't be able to see if it could have gone any further. The downside of becoming a darn good detective and tying up the case yesterday is also proving that the murders in the UK and America aren't linked. Fiona and I will never be Sherlock and Watson.

She emerges from the Del Mar hotel looking radiant in a bright red silk jacket and matching slim pants. Her black hair gleams under the bright Southern California sun. She is positively glowing. Winning a case suits her. I'm happy to have my partner back again, even if it is only for an hour.

I stop the car in front of her and race over to open the passenger door. "I believe you need a ride to the airport." Taking her roller bag out of her hand, a spark of attraction hits me yet again. Placing the roller bag in the trunk, I dread the moment I have to say good-bye.

Fiona settles into the passenger seat and gives me one of her brilliant smiles as I start the engine. Her Shalimar perfume fills the car even though I have the air conditioning on.

As I turn onto the 405 freeway, she says, "I tried to convince my superiors to let me stay a bit longer, but I'm needed back in London right away. I have another unusual case to solve."

I wish I was the one who was going to help her solve it. "A detective's work is never done."

She sighs. "So true." She brushes my hand that is resting on the console. "It has been a pleasure working with you, Derrick." Her smile fades. "I'm going to miss you. My partner in London is a cantankerous coffin dodger."

I laugh at her description, but my gut tells me the man in question is not old, but more than likely the total opposite. He's probably some hunky upper crust British prep school guy who's seeking revenge against his overbearing father by becoming a detective. I appreciate that she doesn't want to hurt my feelings. "Well, I'm glad you got to experience someone a bit closer to your age."

Her musical laugh fills the car and I wish the ride to LAX took two hours instead of forty minutes.

She reaches over and squeezes my hand. "I'll never forget how you saved my life—never."

I want to tell her I will never forget her, but it will sound too much like a romcom line. "It was just instincts and a little magic. Besides, I can say the same about you. Without your shifter skills I might not be driving you to the airport right now."

The serious look on her face remains. "That is a horrible thought." She leans over, brushes my hair off my forehead and gives me a warm kiss that I wish desperately were on the lips. "The world wouldn't be the same without you."

The warmth of her lips on my forehead lingers as I merge into the carpool lane. I can't help but notice the traffic to the airport is lighter than usual. I give her a quick smile, feeling slightly embarrassed by her compliment. "Thanks." I point out the window feeling the need to change the subject. "Looks like the traffic gods are on our side. Is your flight still on time?"

She pulls out her phone and scrolls through her apps. "According to British Airways, my eleven-thirty flight is on schedule."

I try not to show my disappointment. Part of me wished for a long delay so we could spend more time together. During the ten days we worked as partners, we had little alone time. She continues scrolling through her phone and I'm glad to see her ex-boyfriend has not begged for forgiveness. She deserves better. If only the better boyfriend could be me.

She glances up from her phone. "Sorry you never got a chance to play tour guide. I would have liked learning more about Los Angeles."

"Maybe you'll come back again." The second I say it I know the odds are beyond slim.

She nods as she looks out the window at a row of palm trees. "Maybe..."

I had so many versions of our final minutes together in my dreams last night—this wasn't one of them. I reluctantly pull up to the International Terminal at LAX. "We made it in record time."

Fiona smiles. "Thanks to your Zoomer skills." She tosses her phone in her Burberry purse and puts on her jacket. "If you're ever in London, please look me up. I can give you the grand tour."

The only tour I want to give her after the promise of her kiss, is one of my heart. I put the car in park and slowly force myself out of the driver's seat. Popping open the trunk, I pull her roller bag out and place it next to her. "You never know. I might end up in London one day."

She squeezes my hand as I pass her the handle of the roller bag. "I'm going to count on it."

Every bone in my body is aching for her to stay, but I know it is not to be. "Thank you for being the best partner anyone could ask for."

She beams. "We made a great team and solved a difficult case. Mr. Bullock certainly likes us. Who knows, we might be partnered up again."

The wind picks up and her long hair waves gently back and forth like a final good-bye. The faint scent of Shalimar drifts past me. As she disappears through the terminal doors, all I can do is hope she is right. That fate finds a way to bring us back together again just like Sherlock and Watson.

THE END

Read more about Derrick's stint as a detective for WI-6 in *Death by Umbrella*.

Karin De Havin
DEATH
BY
UMBRELLA
THE DERRICK
DUNNE WIZARD
DETECTIVE
SERIES
Book
2

THANK YOU FROM THE AUTHOR

Thank you for reading *Death by Carrots*, book one of *The Wizard Detective Derrick Dunne Series*. I appreciate you taking time out of your day to read my book. I love writing fantasies and paranormal romances and it's because of people like you that I have my dream job. I'm eternally grateful.

I sincerely hope you enjoyed reading this book as much as I enjoyed writing it. If you did, I would greatly appreciate a short review. Even just a line or two can make a huge difference. Reviews help readers discover new authors. I appreciate your support it means a lot!

KARIN'S SERIES
**INDICATES FINISHED SERIES **

If you like Harry Potter with genies, read…
The Genie Academy**
If you like Twilight with wizards, read…
The Girl Chameleon**
If you like The Hunger Games set in Heaven, read…
Nine Lives Part One**
If you like Buffy the Vampire Slayer, read…
How to Snag a Shifter**
If you like books set in foreign lands with ghosts, read…
Tokyo Academy-First Contact**
If you like happily ever after time travel romances, read…
Jin in Time Part One**
If you like books that take place in the world of celebrities and fashion with a fantasy twist, read…
Celebrity Witch**

ABOUT THE AUTHOR

Karin De Havin writes action-packed fantasy, and paranormal romances with kick-ass heroines who love showing villains who's boss. Writing is Karin's dream job.

Karin De Havin is known for her unique books that explore celestial worlds, time travel with a Victorian genie, follow the life of a human chameleon, attend the Genie Academy class of 1890, and travel to Tokyo and learn that ghosts are real.

Find out more about her books at her website www.karindehavin.com. Follow her on Facebook, Instagram, and Pinterest.

Join Karin's newsletter for book inspired recipes in the *Baking with Books* segment and receive a free short story!

Click here to join Karin's newsletter!